CUMBRIA LIBRARIES

3 8003 04831 0825

KT-491-414

BEAKY MALONE

WORST EVER SCHOOL TRIP

For Jane Harris, editor extraordinaire
~ Barry Hutchison

For my parents Dawn and Dave,
even though they never bought me a Furby
~ Katie Abey

STRIPES PUBLISHING
An imprint of the Little Tiger Group
1 The Coda Centre, 189 Munster Road,
London SW6 6AW

A paperback original
First published in Great Britain in 2017

Text copyright © Barry Hutchison, 2017
Illustrations copyright © Katie Abey, 2017

ISBN: 978-1-84715-775-1

The right of Barry Hutchison and Katie Abey to be identified as the
author and illustrator of this work has been asserted by them in
accordance with the Copyright, Designs and Patents Act, 1988.

All rights reserved.

This book is sold subject to the condition that it shall not, by
way of trade or otherwise, be lent, resold, hired out, or otherwise
circulated without the publisher's prior consent in any form of
binding or cover other than that in which it is published and
without a similar condition including this condition being
imposed upon the subsequent purchaser.

A CIP catalogue record for this book is available
from the British Library.

Printed and bound in the UK.

10 9 8 7 6 5 4 3 2

BEAKY MALONE

WORST EVER SCHOOL TRIP

BARRY HUTCHISON

ILLUSTRATED BY KATIE ABEY

Stripes

LEARNING LAND
SCIENCE SHAKE DOWN
BUG'S EYE VIEW
VOLCANO OF THINGS
WHEEL OF ASTRONOMY
Clumso's Railway
times table travel
2x2=4
GRAVITY DROP
circle of squares
CLOSED DUE TO LOW ATTENDANCE
WHERE ART THOU ART?
THERE it is

CHAPTER 1
THE PERMISSION SLIP

It was morning break and I'd spent most of it hiding out from … well, pretty much everyone really. I was sitting on the back bumper of the school minibus, tucked out of sight, when my best mate, Theo, popped his head round the side.

"There you are," he said, spraying crumbs everywhere as he munched on a slice of toast. A slice of toast I knew could only have come from one place.

"Did you go to the canteen?" I asked.

Theo nodded as he crunched away.

"Was Miss Gavistock there?" I asked.

Theo groaned. "Not this again."

Miss Gavistock was one of the school dinner ladies. I'd owned up to fancying her a few days ago and kept bringing it up at every opportunity – despite trying very hard not to.

"I want to marry that woman," I continued. "I'll make her dinner every day and serve it to her on a dirty plastic tray. While scowling angrily, just like she does. How we'll laugh!"

"What are you talking about? Shut up!" Theo said. "Stop going on about Miss Gavistock. It's weird."

The bell rang. I stood up and we both shuffled towards the school's front door, hanging back so I didn't accidentally start talking to anyone.

"I know, but I can't help it!" I reminded Theo. "Trust me, I don't want to say about ninety-nine per cent of the stuff that comes out of my mouth these days."

The truth is, it had been ninety-two hours since I'd last told a lie.

Before then, I'd been something of a lying expert. If they gave out black belts for telling fibs, I'd have been a seventh Dan master. All that changed, though, when I stepped inside a rusty metal box that turned out to be the world's only truth-telling machine. I haven't been able to utter a single lie since.

It was Wednesday morning now and I'd survived two full days of school with only three light beatings from my classmates, two tellings-off from teachers and one wedgie from Helga Morris in the year above. Everyone says you should always tell the truth but it turns out that, when you do, it can get you into all sorts of trouble.

It's amazing, for example, how much offence people take when you remark on their bad breath and body odour. Particularly if they're your head teacher, and they're giving an assembly at the time.

And you're standing on a chair, shouting.

See, being unable to lie isn't my only problem. Whatever that box did to me, it means I struggle to keep the truth *in*. It's like it's always there, waiting to come out at the worst possible times. I can be sitting quietly doing my work when I'll announce out of the blue that I'm planning to copy the person sitting next to me or that I've just stuck a particularly sticky bogey under my desk.

BOGEY

Luckily I sit next to Theo in most of my classes. Theo knows all about my lack of lying ability and is great at helping me cover it up – even though I've accidentally announced pretty much every secret he's ever told me, including the one about him being born with six nipples, four of which had to be surgically removed when he was two.

Especially that one, in fact.

Anyway, like I was saying, it was Wednesday morning. Theo and I made it to the next lesson and I forced my mouth to stay shut as we took our seats.

"You're late," said the teacher, Mrs Dodds, peering at us over the top of her half-moon glasses.

"I walked very slowly," I confessed. "On purpose."

Mrs Dodds's face darkened. She removed her glasses and placed them on her desk. "Is that a fact?"

"Yes," I confirmed. I bit my lip but it didn't help. "I deliberately walked much slower than everyone else, just so I'd be late."

Theo raised a hand. "I tried to hurry him along."

"No, he didn't," I said.

"I did a bit," said Theo weakly.

I shook my head. "He really didn't."

"D'you know, you've just reminded me, Dylan," said the teacher. "I've got a bone to pick with you."

Most of the class had already been looking at me, but suddenly I was the centre of everyone's attention. I shifted nervously in my seat. "Oh?" I asked, the words bubbling up inside me. "Is it about the time I wrapped your car in clingfilm?"

Mrs Dodds gasped and her eyes widened. "That took me hours to get off. That was *you*?"

"Yes. And Theo," I said, jabbing a thumb in his direction. "He helped, too."

"Oh, thanks a bunch, Beaky," Theo muttered.

Mrs Dodds squinted at us both. "We'll discuss that later," she said, her voice ice-cold. "What I was going to say is, you haven't handed in your homework."

"Oh, that. Yeah. My dog ate it," I said.

The teacher sighed. "Your dog ate it? Seriously, that's the best you could come up with? Do you think I was born yesterday, Dylan?"

"But it's true!" I protested. "My dog really did eat it."

"Dogs don't eat homework!" Mrs Dodds snapped.

"You've never met my dog," I told her. "He'll eat anything. Leave him alone with the TV for too long and he'll have a go at eating that."

Some of the rest of the class sniggered at that but I was being serious. Destructo was a Great Dane with an even greater appetite. He ate more food in a day than the rest of the family got through in a week, but he was always scavenging for anything else he could gobble up. That included my homework, my pencils and, on one memorable occasion, my school bag.

"And what about your permission slip for the school trip?" Mrs Dodds asked, arching one of her grey eyebrows. "I suppose the dog ate that, too?"

"No," I said, shaking my head. "My sister stuffed it into my mouth when I posted a picture of her toes on Instagram."

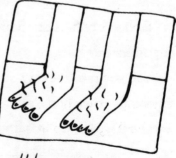

The teacher just stared at me in silence.

"She's got really hairy toes," I explained. "Like a troll."

#hairytrollfeet
#mysisterstoes

The class giggled. Mrs Dodds glanced around, clearly worried that everything was about to erupt into chaos, like it usually did.

"Here, look. I'll show you," I said, reaching for my phone.

"That won't be necessary," she said quickly. "Now, everyone get back to work. Dylan, you can pick up another permission slip at the end of the lesson." She leaned forwards in her chair, clasping her hands together on the desk. Her mouth curved into a thin smile. "But if you don't get it signed by a parent and back to me before the end of lunch, you can forget all about going to Thrillworld tomorrow."

Theo and I stood in the canteen queue, clutching our empty trays and shuffling forwards every few seconds. I had made it all the way to the dining hall without insulting anyone, and while that was something to celebrate, I was too busy thinking about the school trip. There was no way I could get the permission slip signed by my mum or dad and back to Mrs Dodds before the end of lunch.

"It's not fair," I muttered. "I was really looking forward to it. I mean, how often do you get to go to an actual theme park with school?"

"Every year," Theo said.

"Yeah, fair point," I admitted, as we advanced another pace.

"Can't you just forge it?" Theo asked.

I stared at him in awe. "Why didn't I think of that?" I said, swinging my bag off my shoulder. "Theo, you're reasonably intelligent!"

"Er ... thanks," said Theo. "Of course, you could

have said 'genius'."

I shook my head and reached into my bag. "Can't lie, remember? And you're definitely not a genius. I mean, you're not even close to a genius. There are probably some species of monkey that—"

"All right, all right," Theo said. "I get the point!"

Setting my tray on the rail, I took out the permission slip and placed it on Theo's tray, which he was holding at just the right height to lean on. "Right, here goes," I said, giving my pen a flourish. I tried to press the point to the paper, but it stopped a centimetre or so away.

"Huh. That's weird," I said. I tried again, but no matter how hard I pushed, I couldn't get the pen to make contact with the paper. It was as if some invisible force was stopping me. I put my left hand on top of my right and tried to force it down. The hand wobbled, but didn't budge.

Theo glanced at the queue around us. "What are you doing, building up to it? Hurry up."

"I … can't…" I groaned, then I had an idea. "Lift the tray a bit."

Theo raised the tray higher. My hand lifted at the same time, keeping the gap between the pen and the page.

"Argh! It's no use," I said. "This stupid not-lying thing won't let me forge it. Here, you do it," I said, holding out my pen.

"I don't know what your mum's signature looks like," Theo pointed out.

"Do my dad's, then," I suggested.

"I don't know what his looks like, either!"

"Sort of a squiggle, then a line. It's a bit rubbish," I said.

"Oh yeah, that's helpful," Theo said. "That's painted a really vivid picture for me, that has."

I sighed and stuck the pen back in my pocket. It was no use. If Theo just guessed my mum or dad's signature, Mrs Dodds would know right away that we'd forged it. "Oh well, looks like I'll be missing out on the school trip after all," I said.

The person ahead of me in the queue moved off to find a table and I found myself at the front. Suddenly the school trip was the least of my problems. There, revealed before me, was an angel.

"Oh great, here we go," Theo muttered.

Even I have to admit that Miss Gavistock the dinner lady isn't what you'd call *conventionally* attractive. She has tattoos up both arms, shoulders like a wrestler and a permanent sneer on her face that makes it look like she's always smelling something unpleasant. And yet, there's something about her that has hypnotized me since I first set eyes on her.

"What do you want?" she demanded, picking up a chipped dinner plate.

I felt the words bubble up in my throat. *You, Miss Gavistock! It's you I want! Yes, you could probably punch your way through concrete and I'm sure I once saw you sneezing into the beans, but I want to marry you, Miss Gavistock! I—*

"He'll just have some chips," said Theo, stepping in front of me before I could utter a word. I leaned past him and opened my mouth to ask for the dinner lady's hand in marriage, but Theo quickly cut me off. "Look, there's Jodie," he said, gesturing over to a table where my big sister was eating her lunch. "Maybe you should go and embarrass her," he suggested. He shot Miss Gavistock a sideways glance. "You know. Before you embarrass yourself."

I smiled gratefully at Theo. Another humiliating incident avoided, thanks to my trusty best friend and sidekick!

"I'm not your sidekick," said Theo.

"Whoops. Did I say that out loud?"

"You're my sidekick, if anything," Theo said.

I patted him on the shoulder. "Right. You keep telling yourself that," I said, then I scurried across the dining hall and sat down directly across from Jodie. She was deep in conversation with two of her friends and groaned when she turned to find me grinning at her. "What do you want?"

"Hi, Jodie," I beamed. "Hi, Jodie's friends whose names I can't remember."

"Anka and Dawn," Jodie said. "Now what do you want?"

My eyes went from Anka to Dawn and back

again. They weren't scowling at me the way Jodie was. In fact, they both looked quite friendly. Which was a shame, because I'd just remembered something.

I clamped my hand over my mouth before I could announce it. Jodie's scowl deepened. "What are you doing?"

"A mmmpf ymm mpppf," I said.

Jodie leaned over and yanked my hand away. "What?"

"I read your diary," I blurted, then I clamped my hand over my mouth again before I could say any more.

"Yes, I know," Jodie growled. "So?"

I motioned towards Anka and Dawn with my head. "A nmmmf abfff tmm."

Jodie looked at me. She looked at Anka. She looked at Dawn. I watched her expression turn from one of confusion to one of horror.

"Go!" she said, pointing away from the table. "Beaky, go! Right now!"

Anka's delicate features twitched into a frown. "What is it?" she asked, in a lilting Polish accent.

"Nothing," said Jodie. She leaned across the table to me. "Beaky, I'm warning you," she whispered. "I will kill you. I will literally kill you dead. With this spoon." She held up a dessert spoon, clutching it so hard her knuckles turned white.

"I don't plan on saying anything," I told her through a gap in my fingers, "but if I do, it's not my fault. You're the one who shoved me into Madame Shirley's machine, remember? You were the one who wanted me to stop lying."

"How was I to know it was going to work?" Jodie hissed. "I thought she was just a crazy old lady."

"She *was* a crazy old lady," I said. "But it still worked."

Anka and Dawn's heads were tick-tocking left and right as they tried to make sense of our conversation.

"Just go, Beaky," Jodie insisted.

I was about to get up when an idea hit me. Maybe Theo didn't know how to forge my mum's signature, but Jodie did.

I pulled my hand down a fraction. "OK, I'll leave, but only if you do me a favour." I slid the permission slip across the table. "I need a signature."

Jodie looked at the slip. "You need Mum or Dad's signature."

"Whichever you can forge," I said, covering my mouth again.

Jodie snorted. "What, and risk getting caught? No chance."

I flicked my gaze across to Anka and Dawn, who both looked thoroughly perplexed now.

Jodie slammed her hand on the slip and pulled it across the table. "Fine!" She took out a pen and squiggled on the paper. "There. Now go."

"Thanks, sis!" I said, uncovering my mouth. I stood up, just as Theo sat down. "Come on, trusty sidekick. Let's find somewhere else to sit."

"Not your sidekick," said Theo, standing up again.

I tried to turn away. I really did. But before I could head for another table, I felt my mouth opening all by itself. I looked at Anka. I pointed to Dawn.

"She kissed your boyfriend," I said. "Twice." My finger swung across to Jodie. "And she knew all about it."

Anka gasped. Dawn began to protest.

I turned to Jodie, who looked like she was about to explode. "Sorry," I mouthed. "Just came out."

I darted away, just as the squealing and hair-pulling started. Despite the violence erupting behind me, I felt much more positive about the world. I had my form signed. I was going on the trip to Thrillworld!

Assuming my sister didn't kill me first.

CHAPTER 2
CRIME AND PUNISHMENT

After lunch – most of which was spent avoiding Jodie – I strode up to Mrs Dodds in the corridor and handed her my signed form. She took it and looked it over with suspicion.

"I don't know how you managed to get this signed so quickly," she said. Her eyes narrowed, but then she shrugged and folded the paper in two. "But fine. You can go."

"Excellent!" I said, punching the air. That was all I'd planned to say, but my mouth kept flapping all by itself. "My sister forged it. It's not my mum's real signature. I'm surprised you were gullible enough to fall for it!"

I forced a smile. "Um, I'd really appreciate it if you ignored all that stuff I just said."

Ten minutes later, Jodie and I sat silently outside the head's office. Mrs Dodds hadn't taken the news of the forgery particularly well and had sent us both to face whatever punishment Mr Lawson saw fit to dish out.

"I am *never* helping you again," Jodie muttered.

"But..."

She held up a finger. "Shh."

"No, but..."

"Shh. Not another word, Beaky, or I swear I'll go and get that spoon."

"What will you do with it?" I wondered.

"Trust me," Jodie said. "You don't want to know."

The office door opened. We both held our breath, expecting Mr Lawson to come charging out like a raging bull, but instead he emerged beaming from ear to ear. A moment later, his son, Wayne, stepped out with his arm round a smaller boy's shoulders. Wayne was smiling just as broadly as his dad, but unlike Mr Lawson, Wayne's smile made him look like a shark who'd just found a tasty new food source.

"Honest, Dad, it's no problem," said Wayne. "I'll be happy to show Duncan around. We're all *very* proud of the school, and it's my absolute pleasure to help him feel a part of it."

30

"He seems nice," Jodie remarked.

"What?" I said, managing to keep my voice to a whisper. "Wayne? You don't know about Wayne?"

Jodie shook her head. "No."

"Wayne Lawson," I said, stressing each word as if it would somehow make her understand. "Wayne pretend-to-be-nice-but-actually-I'm-a-violent-psychopath-who-wants-to-kick-your-head-in Lawson? You've never heard of him?"

"No, why would I have?" Jodie said. "He's in your year. Why would I care who he is? I barely care who you are."

"Well, he's not nice," I whispered. "Like, at all."

Wayne walked past us, practically dragging the much smaller Duncan along the corridor. "Come on, Duncan, let's start by checking out the toilets," he said, squeezing the boy's shoulders so hard I thought his head might go pop. "Head first," he added, in a voice too quiet for his dad to hear.

Mr Lawson smiled proudly as he watched his son and the new boy head off along the corridor. When he looked down at us, though, his smile fell away completely. "You two. My office," he barked, stepping inside. "Now."

Jodie led the way and I trudged behind her, preparing myself for whatever fate had in store. Whatever it was, it was probably better than poor Duncan's. Just before I entered the office, I glanced along the corridor in time to see Wayne violently shoving the smaller boy through the double swing doors.

"Leave the talking to me," Jodie whispered as we lowered ourselves into the two seats already positioned in front of Mr Lawson's desk.

The head eyed us suspiciously. "What did you say, Jodie?" he asked.

"She said I should leave the talking to her. In case I say something that gets us into even more trouble," I replied. "By the way, your son is really horrible."

"I beg your pardon?" Mr Lawson said, his eyes narrowing to slits.

Jodie tried to laugh it off. "He doesn't mean that. I'm sure Wayne's..."

"Psychotic?" I guessed, filling in for her. "Dangerously unhinged? A two-faced big—"

"Great!" Jodie said. "I was going to say I'm sure he's great."

"He definitely isn't," I corrected. "Didn't you listen to what I said outside? He's a monster."

"Shut up, Beaky," Jodie said, keeping her smile fixed in place.

Mr Lawson looked irritated. "Leaving all that aside ... Mrs Dodds has told me about this forgery thing, and – frankly – I'm very angry at you both."

He looked at us in turn. "Beaky ... I mean, Dylan," he said, correcting himself quickly. "I expected this of you. From what Mrs Dodds tells me, lies, fantasy and make-believe are the norm where you're concerned. I mean ... the dog ate your homework?"

CERTIFIED HOMEWORK EATER

"It's true!" I protested. I gestured up at the books lining the office wall. "I'll bring him in. He'll munch through all this lot given half a chance."

"Enough, Dylan," Mr Lawson said.

"He'd probably have the computer as well, if you left him long enough," I continued.

Mr Lawson slapped the flat of his hand against the desk, making both Jodie and me jump. "I said that's enough!"

I swallowed nervously. "You can be dead scary when you want to be," I muttered.

The head just glared at me, his hand still pressed flat against the desktop. A vein pulsed at the side of his head, as if his whole skull was getting ready to explode. I bit my lip, trying to stop anything else coming out of my mouth, but I was fighting a losing battle.

"You've got one eye bigger than the other," I croaked.

Mr Lawson's face went red with rage. For a moment, I thought he was going to leap across the desk and make a grab for me, but he took a few deep breaths and seemed to bring his temper 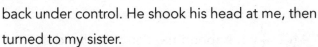 back under control. He shook his head at me, then turned to my sister.

"I expected more of you, Jodie. This isn't like you at all," he said.

"Are you kidding?" I snorted. "She's way worse than me!"

"Beaky, shut up," Jodie hissed.

"That flood in the downstairs girls' toilets last year? That was her," I said. "That time someone dropped an egg from the third floor on to Miss Wilkins? That was her, too."

It was Jodie's turn to be on the receiving end of Mr Lawson's squint-eyed stare. "Is this true, Jodie?"

Jodie frowned and shook her head. "Erm ... absolutely not," she said, doing a sort of puzzled smile that tried to suggest I was a raving madman. "I don't know what he's on about. Eggs? No idea."

The head sighed and leaned back in his chair. "Lies upon lies upon lies," he said. "Do you realize how dangerous what you did is?"

36

"What, dropping eggs on Miss Wilkins? I know," I said. "Shocking."

"Forgery," said Mr Lawson. "Pretending you had permission to go on the trip. What if your parents don't want you to go? Hmm? We can't take you out of school without their permission. They could sue! And we wouldn't want that, would we?"

"No," said Jodie.

"Yes," I said. "Then we'd be rich."

Mr Lawson shook his head as he leaned forwards again. "You've both let me down, you've let the school down and –" he held up his hands – "you know what? I'm going to say it. You've let yourselves down."

MAKIN' IT RAIN!

He gave us a moment for that to sink in. "Do you know who George Washington is?" he asked, once he'd given us enough time to feel ashamed, or whatever else he was hoping we'd feel.

"Is he the guy who runs the carwash near the hospital?" I asked. "With the stoop and the wooden leg?"

Mr Lawson looked confused. "No."

"Oh. What's his name, then?" I asked.

"What? How should I know?"

"Well, you're the one who started talking about him," I pointed out.

Mr Lawson frowned. "About who?"

"George Washington," I reminded him.

The head looked completely lost now. "Yes, but... I mean... What's that got to do with a carwash?"

I shrugged. "You tell me."

"He was an American president," Jodie said.

Mr Lawson half-smiled with relief as Jodie steered him back on to more familiar ground. "Yes. That's right. He was the first president of the United States. And do you know what he's most famous for?"

"Being the first president of the United States?" I guessed.

The head opened his mouth, then hesitated. "Well, yes. That. But he's famous for something else, too. He's famous because – unlike you, Dylan – he couldn't tell a lie."

Jodie and I exchanged a glance, then both leaned forwards in our seats. "Seriously?" I said.

"Couldn't or wouldn't?" Jodie asked.

"Couldn't. So the story goes, anyway," said Mr Lawson. "He was unable to utter a single untruth. I want you to imagine that, Dylan, just for a moment. Difficult for you as it may be."

"Trust me," I said. "It's not that difficult."

The head clasped his hands in front of him and shot me a smile. "And then, when you've contemplated the importance of telling the truth, I want you to write a three-thousand-word report on George Washington by this time next week."

"Ha!" said Jodie.

Mr Lawson shifted his gaze to her. "Both of you."

Jodie spluttered. "What! But..." She glared at me and snarled.

I raised my hand. "Yes, Beaky?" Mr Lawson grimaced. "*Dylan.* Yes, Dylan?"

"Can I copy hers?" I asked, pointing to my sister.

"You can, but you'll be expelled," replied the head. "Any other questions?"

I raised my hand again. Mr Lawson sighed. "What now?"

"In the story about George Washington..." I began.

"Yes?"

I shot Jodie a sideways glance. "Was there ever any mention of an old woman with a big metal box?"

CHAPTER 3
PARENTS' EVENING

Jodie and I sat at opposite ends of the dinner table, with me doing my best to avoid meeting her eye. Every time I looked up from my lasagna I caught her glaring at me and gripping a spoon in a worrying way. Luckily Mum and Dad were sitting between us, so if push came to shove I could use them as human shields to buy myself time to escape.

GRR...

WHIMPER

"This is good," said Mum, shoving a forkful of lasagna into her mouth. She'd been visiting a friend all afternoon, which had meant Dad had been left in charge of dinner duty. "Did you make it yourself?"

Dad nodded proudly. "I did. I followed the recipe to the letter."

Mum looked impressed. "Looks like I've got my very own Masterchef!"

"It was nothing," said Dad. He cleared his throat grandly. "Peel back film lid. Place in microwave. Heat on high for six minutes. Try not to burn your mouth off."

"Oh," said Mum, looking slightly deflated. "It's a ready meal?"

Dad nodded. "It's the one I wrote the jingle for a few months back, remember? They sent me a box of them."

"Was that the racist jingle?" I asked.

Dad scowled. "It wasn't racist. Those were *funny* Italian accents." He waved a hand above his head

like a flamenco dancer and began to sing: "If you-a like-a pasta quick, and a-cheese don't make you sick—"

"You're right, they *were* funny," I said, interrupting him. "If you're a massive racist."

"Can we stop saying your dad's jingle was racist?" said Mum. "Italians do actually wave their arms about and shout 'Mama Mia!' a lot. That's not racist, that's a fact."

"You know who *wasn't* racist? Former US president, George Washington," I said. I looked at my parents hopefully. "Or was he?" I asked. "Any ideas? It'd be really helpful and would save me having to do any research."

"Nice try, Beaky," Jodie growled.

Mum tutted. "Stop calling your brother 'Beaky'," she said. "How many times do I have to tell you? Just because his nose is a little on the large side…"

"It's a *lot* on the large side," Jodie said. "It's like

the rest of his face is attached to *it*, instead of the other way round."

Mum shook her head, annoyed. "Why do you want to know about George Washington?" she asked me.

"We have to do a project on him this week," Jodie said, before I could jump in.

"Both of you?" asked Dad. "But you're in different years. How have you got the same homework?"

"It's not really homework, it's a punishment. Jodie forged your signature at school today," I explained, despite trying very hard not to.

Mum gasped and glared at Jodie. "You did?"

"He made me do it!" Jodie replied.

"That is true," I agreed.

"Well, you couldn't have made a very good job of it, if you got caught," Dad said.

"Actually, the teacher fell for it," I said. "But I owned up."

"Well, good for you, Dylan," said Mum.

"What?" Jodie spluttered. "It was all his idea!"

"Again, that's true," I said.

"She fell for it?" said Dad. He nodded approvingly. "Impressive. Can you do mine, too?"

"A two-year-old could do yours," I pointed out. "It's literally just a line."

"No, it isn't," said Dad defensively. "It's got a blip at the start."

Mum cleared her throat noisily, catching Dad's attention. "I think we might be getting sidetracked, don't you?"

"What? Oh, yes." Dad gave a half-hearted wag of his finger. "Don't do it again."

Mum rolled her eyes. "Well, that showed them," she said. She shook her head at Jodie and me. "I don't know what you were thinking. Still, we'll find out tonight."

"Tonight? Why, what's tonight?" I asked, sipping my glass of milk.

Mum reached for the bowl of garlic bread and helped herself to a piece. "Parents' evening."

I spluttered, spraying the drink all the way across the table. For a fleeting moment I saw Jodie's expression twist into one of horror, then the milk splattered across her face. She sat there, the liquid dripping off her nose and chin, breathing heavily.

"That was an accident. I did not mean that," I said. "I mean, it was hilarious, obviously, but it was completely unintentional."

Jodie made a dive for me, scattering the plates. At the sound of the rattling crockery, Destructo leaped to his feet. Unfortunately he was under the table at the time and as his massive head slammed into it, the whole thing lurched to the left. Mum and Dad made grabs for their drinks glasses, catching them just as the lasagna, garlic bread and a good half a litre of milk toppled on to the floor.

Everyone stopped and stared at the carnage on

the carpet. Everyone, that is, except Jodie, whose hands were suddenly round my throat, squeezing hard, and Destructo, who immediately started to tuck into the lasagna.

"First you make Anka and Dawn start fighting, then you get me into trouble, *then* you refuse to do my stupid report—"

"N-not my fault. Couldn't do it," I wheezed. Under protest, I'd tried to do Jodie's report for her, but just like with the permission slip, my hand refused to write. Doing her work for her would have been a sort of lie which, thanks to Madame Shirley's machine, was now out of the question.

"And *then* you spit milk in my face!" Jodie

snarled. "I'm going to kill you!"

"That's enough!" snapped Mum, dragging Jodie off me.

"It's completely my fault! I started it!" I cried. I played the words over in my head again, then clenched my fists in frustration. "That's not what I meant to say. At all."

"Dylan, get your jacket, you're coming to parents' evening with me and your dad."

I groaned. "Do I have to?"

Mum tapped her foot. "No. No, you can stay here with your sister, if you like. Alone."

I glanced into the dark slits of Jodie's eyes. If looks could kill, I'd have been dead and buried. In an unmarked grave. With a stake through my heart.

"Uh, no thanks," I said, a little more high-pitched than I'd intended. "I'd rather go to parents' evening than be on my own with Jodie!"

Mum jabbed a finger at the mess on the carpet.

"I want all this cleared up before we get back," she told Jodie.

"At least the dog's eaten most of the food," I said, watching Destructo wolf it all down. There was a loud crunch. "And one of the plates."

Dad patted Jodie on the shoulder. "Good luck," he said, then he picked up his car keys, grabbed his coat, and the three of us headed to school.

I sat at the back of the class as Mum and Dad huddled down the front with Mrs Dodds. From the way she was keeping her voice down, it was clear she didn't want me to hear what she was saying. However, the acoustics in the room meant I could hear every word. Not that I really wanted to. She wasn't exactly giving a glowing report.

"Do you know what Dylan's biggest problem is?" Mrs Dodds asked.

Dad looked at Mum and puffed out his cheeks. "Goodness. Where to start? Laziness?"

"Lack of respect for adults?" Mum guessed.

"Poor attention span?" Dad hazarded.

"Complete lack of motivation?" said Mum.

"Lying," said Mrs Dodds. "He's constantly telling lies."

"That's not true!" I called from the back. All eyes turned to me for a moment, then Mrs Dodds lowered her voice even further, but still not enough that I couldn't hear.

"Do you know what he told me today? That the dog ate his homework," she said. She leaned back in her chair, as if her point had been proven. "I mean, honestly."

Mum nodded. "The dog probably did eat his homework, to be fair. The dog eats a lot of things. It was halfway through a serving dish when we left."

"A stainless-steel one," Dad added.

Mrs Dodds blinked in surprise. "Oh. I see. Really? Well, the point still stands," she said, rallying quickly. "He's constantly telling lies and it's not acceptable."

Dad shifted in his seat and glanced back at me. He shot me a reassuring smile, then turned back to the teacher. "He's just got a good imagination, that's all. They're not really lies so much as ... stories. He's creative." Dad pushed back his shoulders, puffing up his chest. "Like me."

Mrs Dodds peered at him over her glasses. "Oh, yes. You write those little radio jingle things, don't you?"

"Not just those," Dad said. "I'm writing a book, too."

"Right. I see. Very good," said Mrs Dodds. She turned to Mum and started to say something, but Dad cut her off.

"Yeah, it's sort of a fantasy adventure, but with kind of romantic science-fiction horror elements," he began. "But, you know, a western. Drama. A western drama. Comedy."

Mrs Dodds raised an eyebrow. "Right…"

"Set in the 1970s," added Dad. "Only not *the* 1970s. A different 1970s. I'd love your thoughts on it some time."

To her credit, Mrs Dodds managed to smile. "That would be lovely."

"Excellent!" said Dad. He reached into the canvas man-bag he'd brought with him, then deposited his manuscript on the desk. All six-hundred pages hit the table with a *thunk*, making the legs wobble. "No rush," he said, beaming broadly. "Just send your thoughts home with Beaky at the end of the week or something."

I could see Mum cringing almost as much as I was. Dad had been writing his novel for what felt like forever and he was always trying to inflict it on some poor unsuspecting test reader.

He'd read the whole thing aloud to the family when Aunt Jas had come to visit and by the end of it I'd wanted to cut my ears off. He'd insisted I give him my thoughts on it and I'd spent the next few minutes explaining just how utterly terrible it was in every way.

Since then Dad had been furiously rewriting it on the computer. Considering it was only two days since he'd started, though, I had serious doubts it was going to be much better. Even Mrs Dodds didn't deserve being subjected to it.

"Run, Mrs Dodds! Run while you still can," I cried.

Once again, all eyes turned to look at me.

"I think," began Dad, "that perhaps Dylan should wait outside."

Ten seconds later, the classroom door closed behind me with a bang. I strolled along the corridor, whistling quietly and spinning the car keys round on my finger. Sitting in the car by myself wouldn't exactly be a barrel of laughs, but at least I wouldn't have to listen to them all talking about me. Or about Dad's book.

I strolled towards the exit, marvelling at how tidy everything looked. They'd really pulled out all the stops to make the place look respectable for the parents. There was no litter or worrying blood stains to be seen, and even the random jackets which had been hanging in the cloakrooms for months had been taken away.

Rounding a corner, I saw a couple of proud-looking parents making their way outside. Wayne held the door open for them.

"Well, thank you," said the dad.

"My pleasure, sir," said Wayne. "Always happy to help."

"Such a lovely young man," the mum said, as she and her husband headed down the steps.

I slowed as I approached the door. Wayne still held it open, but the simpering smile had gone from his face, replaced by the sneer he wore whenever there were no grown-ups around to see.

"Well, hurry up then," he barked. "Are you leaving or what?"

Nodding, I picked up my pace and hurried for the exit. Just as I got there, Wayne let go of the door and it slammed into me. I stumbled backwards, clutching my nose.

"Ow! Dat hurt! I think you broke it!" I protested.

Wayne cracked up laughing.

"Bullseye!" he said, then he put on a show of looking concerned when another parent passed us on the way to the exit.

"Are you OK, Dylan?" Wayne asked, as the woman walked by. "That was quite a knock you took. On your massive nose," he added, when the parent had left. "You're lucky you didn't break the door."

"My nose is bigger than average," I admitted, rubbing it tenderly. "But at least it's honest."

Wayne snorted. "You have an honest nose?"

"I've got an honest everything," I said. "Unlike you."

Wayne stepped closer and eyeballed me. He's

only a little taller than me, but he still manages to give the impression he could snap you in half any time he wanted.

"What's that supposed to mean?" he growled.

There was a very good chance that the next words out of my mouth would be my last, so I tried my best to keep them from escaping. Unfortunately my best wasn't good enough. Try as I might to stop them, the words tumbled out all on their own.

"You're a bully when there are no adults around but too much of a coward to show the real you when there are," I announced.

"What did you say?" he demanded.

"If I had to guess, I'd say you resent all the other kids for taking away your dad's attention, so that's why you're always trying to punish them," I continued, despite the voice at the back of my head shouting, *Shut up, shut up, shut up!* over and over again. I smiled weakly. "But, you know, I'm no expert. And even if that is true, it's completely understandable..."

WHAM! Wayne drove a punch into my stomach, doubling me over. I steadied myself on the wall, half expecting my lasagna to come back up and splatter all over Wayne's shoes.

Part of me would have quite liked that, actually.

"You'd better stay out of my way, Malone," Wayne warned. "And if I hear you've been lying to people and telling them I've got –" he scowled – "*daddy issues*, then I'll make you wish you'd never been born. Understand?"

I nodded. "Understood," I wheezed. "Yep, definitely understood."

"Say it," Wayne snarled. "Promise me you're not going to say anything."

"I'd love to," I said. "But I can't."

Wayne frowned. "You what?"

"I can't promise I won't say anything," I said truthfully. "Because I probably will."

Wayne stepped in closer, drawing back his fist. I braced myself for another bash on the nose, but then Mum and Dad appeared round the corner and Wayne stepped back.

"I'll get you later, Malone," Wayne said, then he changed his expression into one of complete innocence and practically skipped past Mum and Dad.

I let out a sigh of relief. I was saved!

"Get to the car, Dylan," Mum snapped. "You're in big trouble."

Or maybe not.

CHAPTER 4

BEAKY THE SPY

I spent the whole car ride home getting an earbashing from Mum and Dad about how I had to apply myself more, how I had so much potential that was going to waste and how – above all – I needed to stop making up stories all the time.

Except in English, where I needed to make up stories more. Then write them down.

By the time we were home, I was beginning to feel like a parrot repeating the same few words over and over. "But it's not fair. I can't lie. I haven't lied since Saturday!"

"Saturday," said Mum. "Remind me, was that the day you told us that castle was haunted?"

"And used to be owned by pigs," added Dad, closing the front door behind us.

"That was in the *morning*," I protested. "I meant Saturday afternoon!"

Jodie looked up from the dining table at the far end of the front room, where she was writing her George Washington report. "You lied every day for years before that," she said. From her tone I could tell she was still angry with me. "Are you really surprised people don't believe you now?"

I slumped on to the sofa and sighed. "But it's not *fair*," I groaned again.

It was ironic, really. I had been an excellent liar just a few days ago. Truly magnificent. Yes, I'd made up some absolute whoppers over the years – how I'd been sent to Earth from a dying

61

alien world; that there was a giant butterfly called Harold living in my shed. But those were just a smokescreen for all the little, convincing lies that had got me days off school, extra helpings at dinner and – after excelling myself one day – a new bike.

I could lie all day long and everyone believed I was telling the truth. Now, when I could only tell the truth, everyone thought I was lying.

"They didn't even believe me when I told them Wayne sucker-punched me in the guts," I said.

"Well, he didn't," Mum said. "Wayne Lawson wouldn't hurt a fly."

"See!" I yelped.

I almost had to admire Wayne. In his own way, he was as good a liar as I ever was. He had all the teachers and parents convinced he was the nicest kid in school, when really he was like one of those Bond villains who pretends to be a friendly businessman, while secretly building a death ray out of a volcano.

I sat bolt upright on the sofa. "Bond villain!" I cried.

Mum, Dad and Jodie all looked at me. Even Destructo looked up from the table leg he was chewing on and tilted his head to the side.

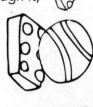

"Goldfinger!" said Dad, in a terrible Sean Connery accent. "Ding! Point to me. Next question."

"What? No, sorry, I didn't mean to say that out loud," I said, jumping to my feet. "Back in a bit," I announced, then I ran upstairs to my room, dragged a cardboard box out from under my bed and tipped its contents on to the floor.

An avalanche of LEGO, broken action figures, coloured pencils, trading cards, bouncy balls and other random rubbish spilled out. I dug through it,

raking at the pile with my fingers, searching for the one tiny chance I had of proving I wasn't a liar.

"Where is it? Where is it?" I muttered, foraging through the old toys.

I pushed aside a Matchbox Batmobile with one of the wheels missing and let out a cry of triumph. There, half covered by a pack of *Top Trumps*, was a button-sized piece of black plastic and glass.

Carefully I picked it up. It didn't look like much but that little gadget was exactly what I needed. I'd begged for a spy camera for months in the run-up to Christmas a couple of years back, only to get bored of it about forty minutes into Boxing Day. Now, though, it was my favourite thing of everything I owned. That little camera was going to change my life.

Before I had a chance to try it out, my bedroom door flew open and Jodie charged in. "You spoke to Michael?" she said, her face stuck midway between anxious and furious.

"Mum said she saw you speaking to Michael from my year."

My heart sank. I'd hoped Jodie wouldn't find out about that.

"I did, yeah," I said. "I bumped into him when Mum and Dad were seeing my music teacher. He'd been at woodwind practice or—"

"What did you say to him?" Jodie demanded.

I swallowed. "Things," I said.

"What kind of things?"

"Just things," I said, trying to sound casual. Maybe I could get away with this. "Things you'd written in your diary," I added, blowing my chances of getting away with anything.

Jodie's fists clenched. "Which *specific* bits?" she hissed through clenched teeth.

"Just about him being in your list of Top Five Boys you fancy, and how you used his cheeks and elbows in a weird Frankenstein's monster-like mash-up drawing that still haunts my nightmares," I blurted out, all in one breath. I smiled weakly.

"That's all."

"That's *all*?" Jodie growled. "That's everything! Now he knows I like him!"

"It's OK, I told him he only scraped on to the list in fifth place," I said. "He looked a bit disappointed actually."

Jodie hesitated. "Did he?"

"Yes," I replied, nodding. "Well, maybe not disappointed," I said truthfully. "What's the word for when you're disappointed, but relieved at the same time?"

Jodie's fingers balled into fists again. "There is no word for that," she said.

"Well, we should make one up!" I suggested, desperately trying to change the subject." *Disalieved. Reappointed.* Or is that already a word?"

Jodie lunged for me, then let out a sharp yelp of pain as she trod on a piece of LEGO with her bare foot. I scrambled up on to my bed, kicking more

of the bricks out between us, forcing her to keep her distance.

"Just wait until I get my hands on you, Beaky!" Jodie snarled.

"I didn't mean to tell him!" I said. "I just couldn't keep it in."

Jodie bent down and started to shove the LEGO pieces aside, clearing a path to me. "I don't want to hear it!" she said.

"You think I do?" I yelped. "You think I want to hear the words coming out of my mouth? You think I want to say these things?"

Jodie hesitated, mid-sweep. "Probably," she said.

"I don't! It's *torture*," I told her. "I humiliate myself a hundred times a day. I'm amazed Theo's still speaking to me, since I've told the world just about every secret he ever shared with me. I can't open my mouth without getting myself into trouble but that's OK because pretty soon no one is going to want to talk to me anyway."

I sighed and slumped back against the wall. "They say honesty is the best policy. Not from where I'm sitting, is isn't." I looked at her and shrugged. "If you want to beat me up, go ahead. It can't make me feel any worse."

Jodie straightened up and folded her arms. "Nice speech," she said begrudgingly.

"Thanks. I've been rehearsing it for just this sort of situation," I admitted, and to my surprise Jodie almost smiled at that.

"I still can't believe you told Michael," she sighed.

"I'm sorry," I told her. "A bit."

For a fleeting second, I thought she was going to try to grab me again but instead she just nodded at the button in my hand.

"What's that?"

I held up the device. "It's a spy camera. I was thinking about James Bond earlier when I remembered I had it. You clip it on to your clothes," I explained, attaching it to my school jumper to demonstrate. "Then it sends video to your phone by Bluetooth."

I opened the app on my phone and held it up. A pixelated version of Jodie looked back at herself from the screen.

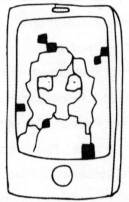

"Oh yeah. I remember that. What did you want it for?" Jodie asked.

"I'm fed up with people not believing me," I told her, sticking the phone back in my pocket. "With this I can record everything. *Everything.* Then, when someone thinks I'm lying, I can play back the footage and prove I'm not."

"Great plan," Jodie said. "Except you can't use it in school. You're not allowed to record anyone or take photos of them without their permission."

I winced. That rang a bell. I vaguely remembered a kid in Year 9 being suspended for taking a photo of one of the teachers smoking in the car park.

"Great," I muttered. I pulled my jumper over my head and dropped it on to my bed. "Well, so much for that plan."

Jodie closed the bedroom door. Against her better judgement, she was clearly feeling sorry for me. "Want to do some lying practice?" she asked.

I nodded glumly. "Yeah. Might as well."

Jodie bent down and picked up a bouncy rubber ball from the mound of toys. "What shape is this?" she asked.

"A sphere," I replied.

"Try again."

"A sphere," I said, then I shook my head. "No, what I'm trying to say is, it's a … a…" I tried to wrestle the word into submission but it was too slippery. "Sphere."

SPHERE
SQUARE
MUFFINS
YOU
CAT
NO!

"Square," Jodie urged. "It's a square. Go on. You can do it."

"Sssss. Sssss," I hissed. I could feel the word "square" inside me somewhere, trapped like a sneeze that refused to come out. I filled my brain with it, reciting it over and over like a chant. *Square, square, square, square.*

"It's a *sphere*!" I yelped. "A three-dimensional geometrical shape with every point on its surface equidistant from its centre!" I drew in a deep breath. "It's no use. I can't do it."

Jodie let the ball drop back on to the floor.

I forced a smile. "Worth a try, though," I said. "Thanks. But it looks like I'm stuck like this, unless we can find Madame Shirley and her shop."

"We'll find it," Jodie said, doing her best to sound convincing. Madame Shirley's shop had vanished shortly after I'd been put through the truth-telling machine, leaving behind only a *To Let* sign and a packet of pickled onion crisps.

We'd gone back a few times since Saturday, trying to find any trace of where Madame Shirley might have gone, but from what we could tell she'd just vanished into thin air, along with her shop, her truth-telling machine and her extensive collection of pickled-onion-flavour potato-based snacks.

"Madame Shirley is definitely the key to turning me back to normal," I said. "We've got to find her, or no matter how much practice I do, I'll be stuck telling the truth forever!"

CHAPTER 5
THE TRAVELLING SHOP

Next morning, I was back to being my positive old self. Mum and Dad had sorted out the permission slip at parents' evening, so I was allowed to go on the school trip after all. A day of zooming around on roller coasters was just what I needed. It was hard to be worried about much else when you were hurtling towards the ground at a hundred miles an hour in a little car.

First, though, there was something else to take care of.

"Whoa, Destructo!" I yelped, half stumbling, half flying along behind the dog. It was my turn to take him for his morning walk but he'd never really grasped the idea that I was supposed to be the one leading the way.

He powered ahead, zigzagging across the pavement, while I had his lead wrapped round my wrist and was frantically trying to keep up.

"Wait! Stop! Slow down!" I yelped as he dragged me across the road. Behind us, there was a screeching of tyres and some angry shouts. "Sorry!" I called over my shoulder.

Destructo panted excitedly as he took a sharp right, dragged me through a hedge and stopped on the pavement on the other side. An old man with a face like over-cooked pastry scowled at us over his fence.

"Oi!" he said. "Are you the one whose dog keeps leaving deposits on the pavement?"

Destructo ran in a circle, sniffing the ground.

"Deposits?" I said. "Like … money?"

"Not that kind of deposit. *Dirty leavings*," the old man said, screwing his face up in distaste. "Soilings. Excrement."

"Oh, you mean does Destructo poo on the pavement?" I asked. "Yes. Definitely. Loads."

"I knew it!" yelped the man. "Why don't you pick it up?"

"Because it's disgusting," I admitted. "Though sometimes I nudge it into the drain with my shoe.

Next time he does it, though, I'll pick it up. I swear."

The old man nodded past me. I turned to see Destructo adopting a squatting position. "Now's your chance," the man said.

"Right. Yeah," I groaned, trying to shut my nose against the smell. "Don't suppose you've got a carrier bag, have you?"

The old man smirked and slowly shook his head.

I sighed. I looked down at the rapidly growing mountain of poo. I flexed my fingers. "Right then," I grimaced. "Looks like we'll just have to do this the old-fashioned way."

"Be through in a minute, just washing my hands," I called from the bathroom, plunging my hands into a sink full of hot, soapy water.

"Hurry up, your cereal's getting all soggy," said Mum.

The cereal could get as soggy as it liked. I took a full five minutes to scrub every millimetre of my hands clean, then dried them off and headed through to join the rest of the family.

Mum, Dad and Jodie were all sitting at the table. Mum and Jodie were both dressed for work and school. Dad, on the other hand, was still in his pyjamas. The radio was playing and Dad was tapping his feet along with the music. Because Dad worked from home, he'd quite often still be in his pyjamas when we all got back to the house in the afternoon. Some people had all the luck.

"How was the dog walk?" Dad asked as I sat down.

"Squidgy," I said. I reached for a slice of toast, stared at my hand for a few seconds, then thought better of it and picked up my cereal spoon instead.

"I want you to be on your best behaviour today, Dylan," Mum warned. "I've promised your teachers you won't get up to any mischief."

"That'll probably backfire," I told her.

"It had better not!" Mum said. "Best behaviour."

"I'll try," I said.

"You'd better try hard. And I don't want you telling any lies today, either. Promise me."

I glanced at Jodie. "That I definitely *can* promise," I said. "I'll do nothing but tell the truth all day."

Mum's eyes narrowed. "Why don't I believe you?" she asked, but before I could answer, Dad jumped up from the table and made a grab for the radio.

"Ooh, this is my new one," he announced. He cranked up the volume and an annoyingly catchy guitar solo blared out. Dad was equal parts embarrassed and proud of every jingle he wrote. He knew they were a bit rubbish but he loved them anyway.

Dad stood in front of the radio, playing air guitar and singing along to the advert's lyrics in a high-pitched heavy metal screech.

"You got an itch on your toes like nobody knows," he sang, thrashing his head to the music. "The skin's blistered and red and sore. It hurts when you walk, but get ready to rock and let Tootsie-Blast settle the score!"

79

He finished with a frantic bit of imaginary fret-bashing as the jingle reached a screeching crescendo, then turned the volume down and took a bow. "I thank you," he said.

"That was … nice," said Mum, taking a sip of her tea. "What was it advertising?"

"Tootsie-Blast," said Dad, sitting down. "Fungal cream for people with manky feet."

"Just what you want to hear someone singing about at breakfast," Mum muttered. She glanced at the clock, then at me. "You'd better go and get your uniform on, Dylan. And remember – best behaviour."

I hurried upstairs, grabbed my tie off the floor and was just wrestling my arms into my school jumper when Jodie's head appeared round the door. "Come here a minute," she said. "I want to show you something."

"Can't it wait?" I asked. "I'm going to be late."

"It'll only take a minute," Jodie said. "Come on. You'll want to see this."

I yanked the jumper over my head and hesitated. "You're not going to beat me up, are you?"

Jodie gave me a look and headed for her room. Fearing a trap, I followed behind at a safe distance. She waited for me to catch up and then pointed to her laptop, which was sitting open on the bed. The moment I saw the image on screen, I felt my heart skip a beat. It was a shop. A shop with a window full of pickled onion crisps.

"Madame Shirley's Marvellous Emporium of Peculiarities," I said in a whisper. "You found it." I touched the screen as if I could somehow reach right inside the picture. "You actually found it!"

"That's the good news," Jodie said.

"What's the bad news?" I asked, getting a nasty sinking feeling.

"*Where* I found it," Jodie said. She clicked and the image was replaced by a city map. I scanned the street names, but didn't recognize any of them. "It's Warsaw," she said.

"I have no idea where that is," I confessed.

"Poland," Jodie said. "It's in Poland."

I stared at the map, then up at Jodie. "Poland? How can the shop be in Poland?"

"Not just in Poland," Jodie said. She leaned past me and flicked through several more images. They all showed the same shop, but with different buildings on either side. "Chicago. Melbourne. Oslo. I even found a reference to it showing up in Pyongyang!"

I looked at her blankly. "Pong-where?"

"The capital of North Korea," Jodie said.

"North Korea?" I stared at the screen, a thousand thoughts racing through my head. "Do they even have pickled onion crisps in North Korea?"

Jodie shrugged. "I guess they do now."

I sat on her bed, my mind reeling. "So ... what does this mean?"

"It means she moves around a lot," Jodie said. "I've found five or six pictures of the shop, even seen it mentioned a couple of times in comments. People saying it was there one day, gone the next. Nothing about the truth-telling machine, though." She opened her mouth to say something else, then closed it again.

"What?" I asked. "What were you about to say?"

Jodie closed her laptop. "Like I say, it looks like she travels around a lot. But the thing is…"

"Yes?" I asked, when her voice trailed off.

She took a deep breath. "The thing is, once she's been somewhere, I can't find anything to suggest that she ever goes back."

My jaw dropped. I stared at her, then at the laptop.

"You disappointed?" Jodie asked.

"Disappointed?" I said. I grinned. "I couldn't be happier!"

Jodie frowned. "What?"

"She exists! She's real!" I cheered. "I was starting to think she was some sort of shared hallucination, but if her shop exists, then Madame Shirley must exist, too!"

"Right," said Jodie, dragging the word out slowly. "But what about the 'never comes back' bit?"

I waved the concern away. "Doesn't matter. We'll figure that bit out." I grabbed Jodie by the arms, surprising her. "But she's real, Jodie! And if she's real then we can find her, and if we can find her then we can change me back!"

I gave Jodie a hug, surprising her even more. Then I spun on the spot and practically skipped out of her bedroom.

We had some leads on Madame Shirley and I was going on the school trip! Yes, I'd started the morning wrist-deep in dog poo, but this was shaping up to be a pretty great day!

Unfortunately it didn't stay that way for long.

CHAPTER 6
THE COACH TRIP

As soon as registration was over, everyone in my year swarmed out to the waiting coaches.

Theo and I clambered on to the first one and made our way to the middle – not too near the front to be mixed in with the nerds, but far enough from the back that we wouldn't be noticed by the hard nuts sitting up there.

Wayne was sitting a couple of rows in front of us, keeping up his nice-guy act for the benefit of the teachers and parent volunteers on the bus. Duncan was sitting beside him, looking like a frightened mouse, squashed in between Wayne and the window. It was odd to see Wayne in the middle of the coach. He wasn't really a middle-of-the-coach guy and should rightfully have been up the back with the hard kids.

Mind you, I couldn't really say anything. If I were being completely honest, Theo and I probably belonged down the front with the nerds. Especially Theo, who was revealing a side to himself I hadn't known existed.

"It's a good coach this," he said.

"Is it?" I asked, glancing around. It looked like any other coach to me.

"Yeah. It's a Journeyman 8228," he said. "You can tell by the shape of the windows."

I looked up at the windows just as the coach pulled away from the school. "They're rectangular.

All bus windows are rectangular."

Theo pointed to the back corner of the window beside us. "Nah, see how it curves in there at the edge? That's how you can tell it's an 8228 and not—"

"That," I said, cutting him off, "is the single dullest sentence I've ever heard you say. In fact," I went on, "it's probably the single dullest sentence I've ever heard anyone say. And considering I've heard my dad read his book out loud, that's really saying something."

"What? It's interesting," Theo protested.

"It really isn't. Why have you never mentioned your interest in buses before?" I wondered.

"It's not a bus, it's a coach," said Theo, lowering his voice. "And, I dunno. I just kept it secret in case anyone made fun of me."

"Theo has a secret interest in buses!" I loudly declared. "He's a closet bus spotter." Around us, some of the other kids began to giggle.

"Thanks for that," Theo said.

"Sorry," I said. "Just slipped out. But keep talking about the windows. With any luck, it might bore me to sleep."

To reduce the risk of my big mouth getting me into trouble, I had decided to try and sleep my way through the journey so I wriggled down low in my seat with my knees on the back of the seat in front.

I spent the next forty minutes trying to nod off. Falling asleep wasn't proving easy though – and not just because of Theo's coach-design insights.

Four different kids were playing four different songs on four different phones, all roughly the same distance away from where Theo and I were sitting. It was like being stuck in the middle of some sort of musical gang war, where the only real losers were Theo and me.

"That's weird."

I opened one eye and looked at Theo. He was gazing out of the window at the countryside whizzing by. "What's weird?" I asked. "If it's about the shape of the windows, I don't care."

"I'm pretty sure we're going in circles," Theo said. "That's the third time we've passed those wind turbines."

I peered past him through the glass. On a hillside a few miles to our right stood several tall windmills with their blades spinning in lazy circles. "They all look the same, though, don't they?" I said.

Theo shrugged. "Suppose," he admitted.

"I doubt we're going in circles," I said. "I'm sure the driver knows where he's going."

"Maybe," Theo said. "But I think something's up."

"There won't be," I assured him. "It'll be fine."

From the front of the bus, there came the sound

of someone loudly clearing their throat. I leaned into the aisle to see Mrs Rose, the deputy head, standing up.

"Attention, everyone. Attention," she said, her shrill voice easily carrying all the way to the back of the coach. "I'm afraid there's been a bit of a mix-up."

"I knew it," Theo whispered. "We're not going to Thrillworld."

"Of course we are," I said.

"I'm afraid we won't be going to Thrillworld," Mrs Rose announced.

GASP

A chorus of gasps and groans and *why nots* rose up from the seats around us. Theo shot me a smug look. "See," he said. "Told you."

WHAT?!

GROAN

"I've just had word that there's been some confusion with our booking for this coach," said Mrs Rose.

"*Someone* at the school office – I won't name any names – didn't book us tickets for Thrillworld. The good news is," she continued, raising her voice to be heard over the uproar, "they did book us tickets for another theme park."

A hush fell as everyone waited to hear where we were going. The staff at the school office always seemed pretty clueless, so it could have been anywhere. Thorpe Park. Legoland Windsor. Disneyland Paris. There was no saying where they'd got us tickets for.

"So hold on to your hats," said Mrs Rose, trying to sound enthusiastic but failing miserably. "We're off to Learning Land!"

That did it. Almost all of the fifty or so kids on the coach erupted and began to shout at the same time. "Learning Land's for eight-year-olds!" cried one.

"The rides are pathetic," complained another.

"And they've got that stupid clown mascot," Theo chipped in.

My eyes went wide. Of course! Clumso the Clued-up Clown. How could I forget about him? He'd come to my primary school once and – like most clowns – I'd found him a bit on the creepy side. My reaction was nothing compared to someone else's, though…

CLUMSO

I straightened up and looked over the top of the seats in front of us. Wayne was sitting bolt upright, completely rigid. It was possible he was trembling, but I was too far away to be sure. It took every bit of my willpower to stop myself laughing.

Wayne had a history with Clumso the Clued-up Clown. Only a handful of my old classmates were likely to remember, and I was sure Wayne would never *ever* want it shared. I'd kept the secret for years, knowing full well he'd kill me if I told anyone.

93

Unfortunately keeping secrets was no longer my strong point.

"Clumso the Clued-up Clown came to our primary school once, and Wayne got so scared he wet himself," I announced in a loud voice. "Right in the middle of the class!"

OH.

There was a moment of absolute silence. Even the drone of the diesel engine seemed to fade away until you could have heard a pin drop. And then the roar of laughter rushed along the coach like a tidal wave, sweeping from the back all the way down to the front.

HA! HA! HA! HA! HA! HA! HA! HA! HA! HA! HA! HA! HA! HA! HA! HA! H

"Oh no," I whispered, as Wayne turned in his seat and threw me a glare so furious it could have shattered concrete. "What have I done?"

"We were in Year One," Wayne growled.

"We were in Year Six," I replied, despite trying very hard not to. "As soon as Clumso came into the class you stood up, burst into tears and peed your pants."

The laughter rose to tsunami levels. Mrs Rose was shouting angrily from the front, but the sound was too loud for even her fingernails-on-blackboard voice to cut through it. I slunk down in my seat, avoiding Wayne's glare.

"That was probably a mistake," Theo said.

"Does he look angry?" I whispered.

Theo shook his head. "No, I wouldn't say that."

I breathed a sigh of relief.

"'Angry' isn't a strong enough word for it," Theo said. "Furious, maybe. Enraged. You know that face the Incredible Hulk does when he's smashing a tank over someone's head? It's a bit like that. But worse."

I buried my face in my hands. "I'm so dead. I am so dead. What's he doing now?"

"He's just sort of glaring at everyone else," Theo said.

As he said it, the laughter began to die away. First, the nerdy kids down the front fell silent, and I could imagine Wayne turning his sneer on them.

The silence rushed along the bus as Wayne fixed all those laughing with his dead-eyed stare. In moments, the uproar had been replaced by a frightened silence.

"Thank you," screeched Mrs Rose. "Dylan Malone, stand up!"

"He can't stand up. Health and safety," said the bus driver. "You shouldn't even be standing up."

Mrs Rose scowled at him and almost said something, then decided against it. "Fine, don't stand up, Dylan, but listen very carefully," she said. "I will not tolerate bullying on this trip."

"Oh, thank God for that," I whispered to Theo. "Wayne might not get a chance to beat me up."

"So I want you to apologize

for bullying poor Wayne," Mrs Rose continued.

I jerked upright, poking my head above the seats. "What?" I spluttered. "Me? Bully *him*?"

"It's completely unacceptable," Mrs Rose snapped. "Wayne was sitting minding his own business, only for you to humiliate him with your nonsense stories. I will not allow it."

She turned to Wayne. He was kneeling on his seat with his back to her, his eyes locked on me like a military targeting system preparing to fire. "Are you OK, Wayne?" Mrs Rose asked.

"I'll b-be fine, Miss," Wayne whimpered, still staring at me. He was scowling so hard his eyebrows had become a single hairy strip, but his mouth was slowly twisting into a grin. "I know Dylan and I could be the best of friends, Miss. If only we had the chance," he said.

Wayne finally turned away from me and looked imploringly at Mrs Rose. "Perhaps we could be partners on the trip."

I felt my blood turn to ice. "No!" I yelped. "That's a terrible idea."

Wayne let his shoulders droop. "Oh well," he said. "If Dylan really hates me that much, then I suppose…" His voice cracked and he dabbed at the corner of his eye with a sleeve. Even I couldn't help but be impressed by his act.

Mrs Rose fell for it hook, line and sinker. "I think that's an excellent idea, Wayne. It'll give you boys a chance to get to know each other better. It's decided," she announced. "Wayne will partner up with Dylan. Theo can go with Duncan."

Duncan's head popped up beside Wayne, like a meerkat looking for danger. A broad smile was plastered across his face and his eyes were little circles of excitement. He gave Theo an overly enthusiastic wave and almost sobbed with relief.

Beside him Wayne slowly turned back to look at me. There was an expression of demented glee on his face. "Thanks, Miss," he said. "I'm sure Dylan and I are going to have a lot of fun together." Wayne winked at me. "We're going to get on like a house on fire."

"Yes," I whispered, swallowing nervously. "He'll be the flames and I'll be all the people running about screaming."

I slumped down in the seat and stared at the traffic whizzing past on the motorway.

"It might not be that bad," said Theo. "Maybe Wayne does just want to be friends."

I met Theo's gaze and raised my eyebrows.

"No, you're right," Theo said. "You're a dead man."

"It's not just Wayne," I whispered. "Without you to cover for me, there's no saying what sort of trouble my truth-telling is going to get me into!"

"Loads, probably," said Theo.

"Exactly."

"I mean, it doesn't bear thinking about."

"That's really not helping." I looked around the coach. "You're an expert on these things," I said. "Does this coach have an escape pod?"

Theo shook his head. "Not that I know of."

"No, didn't think so," I said glumly. I went back to staring at the passing traffic, part of me wishing I hadn't managed to get that permission slip signed after all.

CHAPTER 7

To anyone over the age of eight, Learning Land isn't so much a fun-packed theme park, as a misery-laden form of punishment. The beauty of theme parks – the whole point of theme parks – is the fast-paced rides that hurtle you around until you throw up.

Learning Land's rides don't make many people throw up, but they've probably made a few people die of boredom. Imagine a theme park designed by a headteacher and you'd be pretty close. Only a *really* dull headteacher who hated theme parks.

And fun. And children.

Mum and Dad had taken Jodie and me there when I was about six and it had very nearly put me off theme parks for life.

There was one roller coaster, which travelled at about four miles per hour and stopped every thirty seconds until someone on board shouted out the answer to a randomly generated sum.

The log flume didn't plunge riders into icy water, but gently glided them down into colourful bubbles. This apparently taught them something about science, but I have no idea what.

Even the sideshow stalls were education-based. Throw a dart at the correct capital city! Hook the reigning British monarch of 1862! Knock down the incorrect letters in these commonly misspelled words! It was dire.

Despite that, there was a massive queue at the gates when we finally arrived. Hundreds of primary school kids were lined up, all waiting to get inside. We towered above them like giants. Every few seconds one of the younger kids glanced nervously at us like we might jump on them and start eating them or something.

"What's the hold-up?" Theo wondered as we waited in line. We'd been queuing for twenty minutes and I'd stuck to Theo like glue. If I had to be partnered up with Wayne, I was going to delay it as long as I possibly could.

I tucked my clipboard under my arm and peered over the heads of the kids in front – which wasn't difficult, as they were all about four feet tall. At the gates, one of the park's staff was interrogating a worried-looking boy.

"It's always slow," I said to Theo. "The gate staff ask you a question before they let you in."

Theo frowned. "What sort of question?"

"A maths question. Or geography. Or something. I can't really remember," I said. "It's part of the whole learning theme."

"I hope I don't get history," Theo said.

"It's for primary school kids. It's not going to be difficult," I assured him, just as another gate opened up.

Everyone from my bus made a run for the new gate, clipboards flapping as we rushed to be the first in line. I've got no idea why we were all in such a hurry, as none of us actually wanted to get inside. It isn't easy to resist a new queue, though.

Theo and I arrived two or three places behind the leaders, who cheered with triumph as the woman on the gate took their tickets.

"Welcome to Learning Land," the woman smiled. She glanced along the queue, clearly surprised by the size of us all. "Get ready to enter our wondrous world of wonder, but before you do ... what's eight plus six?"

"Fourteen," said the girl at the front. The staff member smiled, then stamped the girl's hand and ushered her through the gate.

"What's the capital of England?" she asked the next kid in the queue.

"London!" the boy replied. He got a stamp, and in he went.

"See? It's easy," I said, as the person in front of us managed to spell 'house' correctly.

The woman turned to me. "Which US president famously couldn't tell a lie?" she asked.

I blinked in surprise. The woman kept smiling at me expectantly. "Um, George Washington," I said. I felt the stamp press down on my hand. The woman gave me a map of the park, then stepped aside to let me through.

"Another history question," she said, turning to Theo.

"Oh. *Yay*," Theo said.

"Name the Prussian chancellor who united the disparate Germanic states in the mid-1800s."

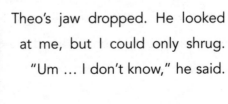

Theo's jaw dropped. He looked at me, but I could only shrug.

"Um ... I don't know," he said.

The staff member smiled at him encouragingly.

"Go on. Have a guess," she said.

Theo puffed out his cheeks. "Brian?" he said. "Brian something?"

"BZZZZZZ!" cried the woman, making half the queue jump in fright. "Wrong! Let's try a different one. Which sixteenth-century poet famously said—"

"I need the toilet," Theo announced, thrusting his hand out towards her.

"No, he doesn't," I said, then quickly clamped my hand over my mouth.

The woman looked Theo up and down. He hopped anxiously from foot to foot. "I'm desperate," he said. "It's going to come out."

She stepped back and hurriedly stamped his hand. Theo dashed through the gate and we walked over to join the rest of our class and wait for the others.

106

"How come I got those questions?" Theo asked. "I got as far as 'name the' on the first one, then she lost me."

"Speaking of losing people," I said. "Let's sneak away before Wayne gets through."

"Could be risky," Theo said.

"Risky?" I yelped. "Not as risky as teaming up with that lunatic."

"What lunatic is that then?" growled a voice right behind me. I froze, too terrified to turn round.

"That's him, isn't it?" I whispered. Theo nodded slowly. "Yeah," I said. "Yeah, I thought so."

I shuffled round in a half-circle to find Wayne grinning. I was sure he was going to lunge at me and mash me into a lumpy paste there and then, but then I saw Mrs Rose approaching and knew I was safe. For the moment, at least.

"Wayne, Dylan, you've found each other. Good," she said. "Theo, Duncan's over there by the bench. Dancing, for some reason. Go and join him."

Theo shot me a concerned look. "Uh, I'll see you at lunchtime," he mumbled. He glanced at Wayne. "Hopefully."

Giving me an encouraging smile, Theo walked over to where Duncan was jigging about merrily on the spot.

Mrs Rose nodded at my clipboard. "Don't forget to write up your report about the trip as you go," she said. "We're not just here for fun, you know."

I glanced around at the tame rides and boring sideshows. "Just as well."

"And remember, Dylan – best behaviour," the teacher said, jabbing a red-polished fingernail in my direction. "This is a great opportunity for you two to become friends. If I hear you've been bullying Wayne, I will *not* be happy. Understood?"

"I'm not going to bully Wayne," I said truthfully.

"I'm sure he won't, Miss," said Wayne.

Mrs Rose smiled warmly at him. "Oh, Wayne. Such a kind, sensitive boy." Her face twisted into a snarl as she turned back to me. "You had better not upset him. Is that clear, Dylan?"

"Yes, but—"

"Good. That's settled, then," she said. She shot me a final warning look then turned to address the whole group.

Mrs Rose was halfway through telling us how we were all ambassadors for the school when Wayne's fingers wrapped round the back of my neck. "Come on, we're getting out of here," he said, his voice a scratchy whisper in my ear.

"I think we should probably stay," I protested, but Wayne half dragged, half shoved me away from the rest of the group and we were soon lost in a crowd of overexcited six-year-olds and their frazzled teachers.

When we were safely out of sight of the others, Wayne steered me down an alleyway between two rows of sideshow stalls. "Where are you taking me?" I asked, suspecting it wasn't going to be anywhere nice.

"To explore the park, of course," he said. "We're going to have lots of fun together today, Beaky. We're going to have a real laugh." He leaned in so close I could smell his stale breath. "Or I am, anyway."

He released his grip, then thrust his clipboard at me. I yelped and held my hands up to shield myself, before realizing he wasn't hitting me with it. "Take that," he said. "You can write my report for me."

I looked down at the clipboard and the lined paper attached to it. "I can't," I said.

Wayne growled. "What do you mean, *you can't?*"

I gulped. "An old woman put me in a magic machine and now I can't tell lies and an invisible force stops me writing stuff that isn't true."

Wayne's eyes narrowed. He looked like he was about to question the story, but then shook his head. "Whatever," he said. "Just get it done. And you can carry my jacket, too."

He tossed his scrunched-up jacket at me then spun round and clapped his hands. "Now, are there any decent rides in this place or what?"

I was about to tell him there weren't, when something caught my eye. It had been a few years since my one and only visit to Learning Land and since then it seemed they'd built a new ride. It rose high above the rest of the park, a teetering tower of metal and glass.

"Gravity Drop," I said, reading the sign mounted on the top of the tower. Right below the sign was a glass elevator. A dozen or so kids stood inside it, all gripping handrails. "I wonder what that one does," I said, then jumped as the elevator dropped and everyone inside it began to scream.

AHHH

The lift hurtled downwards at breakneck speed, and I was convinced it was going to smash into the ground. Just before it did, though, there was a hiss of hydraulics and the elevator slowed to a gentle stop. The doors opened and the children raced out, laughing and whooping with delight.

I glanced at Wayne. "That one looks pretty exciting," I said. "Too exciting, if anything."

Wayne shifted uneasily. He licked his lips, which suddenly looked very dry. "What, that thing? Nah. That's well tame. Besides, the queue's probably massive."

I peered over at the ride entrance. "There's no one there," I said.

Wayne rounded on me. "I said we're not doing it, all right?" he growled. "That's a baby's ride. For babies. Do I look like a baby to you?"

"No," I said. "But didn't your mum make you wear pull-ups for a fortnight after you wet yourself?"

"Have you got a death wish or something?" Wayne snarled, suddenly right in my face again. As he drew back his fist there was a flurry of movement behind him, followed by a loud *honk* and a high-pitched laugh that made Wayne's face turn ash-grey.

"Crack a smile, wipe away that frown, have some fun with this clued-up clown!" giggled a voice.

Slowly Wayne lowered his fist and turned. A tall figure with curly orange hair and a shiny green outfit leered at us from behind a red nose. He jigged towards us, his massive shoes flapping noisily on the ground, his pom-pom buttons bouncing up and down.

"I'm the hip, cool clown with the clued-up act," Clumso sang, his mouth fixed in an impossibly wide grin. "Now pin back your ears and I'll give you a fact!"

Wayne tried to dodge past but Clumso blocked his path. The clown's face was painted white, with rings of purple and green round his eyes. "Not so fast, young man!" Clumso said, still giggling. I had to admit, I could almost see why Wayne's bladder control had failed him last time. Clumso was pretty creepy up close.

"Learning Land's not just for fun, so hear my fact before you run!" Clumso said. His rhymes were so rubbish, I was starting to wonder if my dad had written them.

"I don't care. Leave me alone, you big freak," Wayne said, trying to get past again.

Clumso blocked his path once more, a flicker of irritation passing behind his face paint. "Well, it's in Clumso's job description," the clown said, the humour going out of his voice. "So just do me a favour and listen, all right?"

His smile returned. "An animal fact, I think I'll reveal!" he began, just as Wayne swung back a leg and kicked him on the shin.

"Argh! You little…" Clumso began, hopping on one massive shoe. Wayne shoved the clown hard in the chest, sending him crashing to the ground.

I glanced around, expecting to find teachers and park security all charging towards us, but no one seemed to have noticed Wayne roughing Clumso up.

"Come on. Run!" Wayne cried, grabbing me by the sleeve. Clumso was struggling back to his feet, his smile now replaced by an angry scowl. Wayne powered forwards, dragging me along behind him.

"Get back here, you little hooligans!" Clumso bellowed, but Wayne had no intention of stopping. We sprinted round a bend and were confronted by a sea of children half our size. Clumso's shoes would slow him down, but we'd stick out like sore thumbs in this crowd.

"We have to hide!" Wayne said, his eyes darting frantically around us. "We have to hide!"

"I'm sure if we just apologize, he'll understand," I said. Wayne looked at me like I'd just suggested impaling a load of puppies on spikes.

"Are you *insane*?" he gasped. He pointed back in the direction we'd come from. "He can't be reasoned with. He can't be bargained with. He doesn't feel pity or remorse or fear and he absolutely will not stop. Ever."

I shot him a doubtful look. "I think you're getting Clumso the Clown mixed up with the Terminator."

"Whatever," Wayne scowled. He was starting to look frantic now. "We need to find somewhere to hide – fast."

"How about there?" I said, pointing to a little train ride a short distance away on the right. There were a few empty carriages sitting on the tracks, all designed to look like individual old-fashioned steam engines. "We could hide in one of them."

Wayne didn't wait to be told twice. He tore off

towards the train, shoving smaller kids out of his way. I ran behind him, apologizing to the six-year-olds that came flying past me.

I caught up with Wayne at one of the empty carriages. He ducked inside, then let out a squeal of panic when he saw the face of Clumso grinning back at him.

"It's just a painting," I said, but then we heard the real Clumso not too far away.

"Where did you go, you little thugs?"

At the sound of the clown's voice, we both ducked out of sight. I had to admit, I was seeing Clumso in a whole new light, and even though I wasn't quite at the peeing-my-pants stage, my heart was racing in panic.

First I'd been partnered with Wayne and now I was being hunted down by an angry, learning-obsessed clown.

"Seriously," I whispered. "Could today get *any* worse?"

Which, in hindsight, was a silly question.

CHAPTER 8

TUNNEL OF TERROR

We kept low, holding our breath, listening for any sign that Clumso had found us. Other than the clatter of the rides and the excited chatter of the younger kids, though, it was hard to hear much of anything.

"Has he gone?" Wayne whispered, after several long seconds had passed.

"Dunno," I said.

"Well look, then," Wayne growled.

"You look," I said, but then Wayne punched me hard on the arm.

"Fine, I'll look," I grumbled. Cautiously I peeped over the top of the carriage.

I could see Clumso in the distance. He was still hunting for us, but was walking in completely the wrong direction.

"It's OK. He's gone," I said. "You can relax."

"I was perfectly relaxed," Wayne said. "What are you trying to say?"

"Nothing, just—"

"Just what?" Wayne demanded. "Are you saying I was scared?"

"Yes!" I cried, despite my best efforts not to. "You were terrified. I thought you were going to wet yourself again."

"I wasn't scared," Wayne said, grabbing me by the front of my school jumper. "I'm not scared of nothing."

Our carriage gave a sudden lurch and Wayne almost jumped into my arms.

"What's happening? Is it Clumso?" he gasped. "It's Clumso, isn't it? We're going to die!"

"The ride's starting, that's all," I said, pushing him off me.

"What? No. I'm not going on a stupid kids' ride," Wayne said, as the carriage clattered slowly round a bend in the track. He moved to climb out, but a member of staff shouted at him from the platform.

"Sit down! Arms and legs inside the vehicle at all times."

"Come on, sit down," I said. "If we're on here there's less chance of Clumso finding us."

Wayne glared at me for what felt like forever, then he sighed, slumped down on to the plastic seat beside me, and fastened his seat belt. "What is this anyway? A roller coaster?"

I unfolded the map I'd been given at the gate and studied it. "Right, so we came in here," I said, pointing to the entrance. "You physically assaulted much-loved children's character Clumso the Clued-up Clown here. This is where you ran in terror."

"*You* ran in terror, more like," Wayne snorted, thumping me on the leg.

"Ow! Meaning this is where we are now," I said, squinting at the ride description on the map. I tried to stop myself grinning, but the urge was too great. "Oh dear," I said, looking up at Wayne. "It's a history of the UK rail network."

Wayne did an exaggerated yawn. "Presented by an animatronic Clumso the Clued-up Clown," I added.

Wayne froze, mid-yawn. The carriage turned another bend in the track, revealing a set of swing doors leading into a tunnel. The entrance had been designed to look like Clumso's laughing face, with the track leading directly into his open mouth.

HEE HEE!

Frantically, Wayne tried to get up, but the seat belt was locked in place and refused to set him free. He gripped the chair's armrests, his knuckles turning white as the swing doors opened and we heard Clumso's high-pitched giggle echo through the darkness.

HEEEE!

The laughter faded and the carriage clattered on through the gloom. Colourful murals of Clumso dressed as a train driver illuminated as we passed them, each one making Wayne recoil in fright.

"You know he's just a guy in a costume, don't you?" I said.

HEE HEE!

"Shut up. I'm not scared," Wayne hissed, then he screamed as a robotic model of Clumso came swinging out from the wall, its arms dangling limply at its sides.

"The first ever locomotive-hauled railway route in the world ran between Stockton and Darlington," the animatronic Clumso announced, his mouth whirring open and closed, completely out of sync with the sound.

Wayne pressed himself back in his seat, trying to put as much distance between himself and the robo-clown as possible. He sighed with relief as we pulled past it, then screamed again when an upside-down Clumso dropped from the ceiling on a spring.

"Three and a half million people travel by rail in the UK every day," Clumso announced. "Making the UK rail network one of the busiest in Europe!"

Wayne ducked as we passed the puppet, briefly covering his head with his hands. He squealed as a steam engine whistled past us in the opposite direction, a dummy of Clumso propped up in the driver's seat.

"Britain's worst rail disaster happened near Gretna Green in Scotland in 1911," echoed Clumso's voice from nowhere. We rounded a corner to see a model of Clumso standing with his hands clasped in front of him, looking down at a gravestone. His red

123

nose had been replaced by a solemn black one. "Over two hundred people died!" continued his disembodied voice.

As we passed the grave scene, the robotic Clumso blew his nose on a spotted handkerchief. It made a sound like a sad trombone.

"This is the worst thing that's ever happened in the world," Wayne whispered. I glanced sideways at him and saw he had his eyes tightly shut.

"I dunno," I said, putting my hands behind my head and leaning back in the seat. "I'm quite enjoying it. It's informative *and* fun. It's *infunmative*."

Wayne opened his eyes just enough to shoot me a furious glare. "I swear, if you tell anyone about this, you're a dead man," he warned, then he closed his eyes again, jammed his fingers in his ears and began to hum.

Eventually, after I'd learned a surprising amount about the UK rail network and Wayne had been mentally scarred for the rest of his life, we got off the ride. Wayne was shaking from head to toe, and his eyes were ringed with red.

"Were you crying?" I asked.

"Of course I wasn't crying!" Wayne said. "It was dusty in there. I'm allergic. All right?" He shook his head and sniffed. "Crying. Ha! As if."

He tapped one of the clipboards I had been left to carry. "Better make a start on my report. Say that ride was lame. Too slow and boring. And if you say anything about me crying I'll kill you." He tapped the board again. "Come on. Chop chop."

"No, but—" I began, but Wayne about-turned and walked off.

"Come on, let's see if we can find somewhere quiet," he said, cracking his knuckles.

"To hang out and chat?" I asked hopefully.

Wayne snorted. "You wish. Report. Get it done."

There was no point trying to explain, so I just shrugged and moved Wayne's clipboard behind mine. Scribbling my name at the top, I began to write up my thoughts on the railway ride. I soon found myself writing a detailed account of every one of Wayne's whimpers and sobs, though. If Wayne saw it, he was sure to kill me, so I put the lid back on my pen and hurried to catch up with him.

We were wandering through a busy area of the park, with lots of little kids and their teachers rushing around. I could see a few of the kids from my school shuffling about looking bored and one or two parent helpers looking even more so. I knew Wayne wouldn't dare attack me there. Not when there was a chance one of the adults might see him.

Wayne had obviously realized he was powerless here, too. He started walking towards a narrow path which a signpost told us led to the *Maze of Maths*. Theoretically it was possible for someone to get lost for days in the sprawling hedge maze – unless

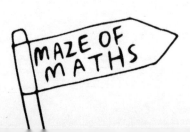

they had a basic grasp of
adding and subtracting,
in which case they'd find their
way out in no time.

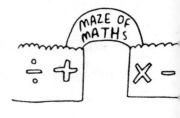

More worryingly, though, the hedges were too high for anyone to see over. Wayne just had to lead me along a few twists and turns and no one would be able to see him beating me senseless.

"We should stay here," I said. "In full view of several adults at all times."

Wayne beckoned to me with one finger. "Move. Now. The longer you make me wait, the worse it'll be."

I started to follow him, dragging my feet along the ground. He was probably right. It was best to get my beating over and done with. I was only delaying the inevitable.

We'd just turned on to the path that led to the maze when I caught a whiff of a familiar smell. I inhaled deeply, trying to work out what it was. It was sort of sweet but sour at the same time.

I'd smelled it recently, I was sure. Not today but within the last week.

"Of course!" I gasped, suddenly realizing what the smell was.

WHAP! Something hit me in the face. I reached up and peeled away an empty bag of pickled onion crisps.

I turned on the spot, looking around, suddenly filled with the sense that I was being watched. I'd been hit in the face with lots of things over the years – pillows, footballs, Jodie's fists – but I'd never had a crisp bag slap itself across the end of my nose. For it to have happened now with a packet of pickled onion – when I only knew one person in the world who liked pickled onion flavour – couldn't just be a coincidence, surely? Or rather – *Shirley*.

I couldn't shake the feeling that not only was I being watched, but that the person watching me was Madame Shirley herself. I didn't know how or why, but I somehow knew she was there in Learning Land. All I had to do was find her.

As I looked around, another breeze whipped up, snatching the packet from my hands. It blew away, hopping and skipping across the ground and weaving around all the other kids.

I glanced back at Wayne. He hadn't noticed I had stopped and was still trudging towards the maze. I watched the crisp bag flutter away in the opposite direction.

And then, after a very brief debate with myself, I ran.

CHAPTER 9
STOMACH SPRAY

"Sorry. Excuse me. Coming through," I said, forcing my way through the throngs of children, teachers and parents. "It's an emergency. I'm chasing an empty crisp packet."

"Oi! Get back here!" Wayne's voice cried out in the distance, but I couldn't worry about that for now. Following the crisp bag was my first priority.

The packet skipped along just above the ground, leading me across the busy plaza. It took a left at the *Wheel of Astronomy* and hung a right at *Bug's Eye View*. I chased it as it fluttered past

the controversial *Get Dem Nazis* ride, which had opened three months ago for just one day, before a record number of complaints saw it immediately shut down.

It wasn't easy to run fast carrying two clipboards and Wayne's jacket. I lost sight of the crisp packet half a dozen times as I chased it but whenever I fell too far behind, I'd find it lying on the path just ahead of me. When I got close, it took off again, and I couldn't help feeling that it had been waiting for me to catch up.

I skidded round another corner, gaining on the floating bag. It looped in the air, then took a sharp left and came to rest on the seat of a waltzers-style ride designed to teach children about centrifugal force and how unpleasant an experience it can be.

Throwing myself into the seat, I made a grab for the packet and caught it just before it could flutter off again. "Aha!" I cried, holding it above my head. "I did it! I caught the crisp packet!"

Around me, in the other cars, several bemused

eight-year-olds looked at me and my crisp bag, then started whispering and sniggering. "I think it's a magic crisp packet, sent by an old woman," I explained, which only made them worse.

"Gotcha!" said Wayne, catching me by the back of the neck. Startled, I let the crisp packet slip from my fingers again.

"No, come back!" I said, making a grab for it, but it fluttered upwards out of reach. I was about to give chase, when a member of staff blocked my way.

"Right, sit down," he said. "Ride's about to start."

I tried to dodge past but Wayne still had his death-grip on the back of my neck, keeping me from moving. He forced me down into the seat. "Let's take the weight off our feet for a while," he said, flashing me his shark-like smile. "Then we'll find somewhere nice and quiet to hang out, just the two of us. Somewhere I can pay you back for that stuff you said on the bus."

"About wetting yourself, you mean?" I said.

The eight-year-olds around us sniggered behind their hands. Wayne shot them a look, but they had no idea who he was and he was powerless against them. They kept laughing as the safety bars lowered over our laps, locking us in place.

One of the younger kids wasn't laughing. She was a small girl with light blond hair and a worried expression. She was in the car directly across from us, sitting all on her own.

"Are you OK?" I asked her.

"I'm just... I'm a bit scared," she said, her voice barely a whisper.

"Yeah, no wonder," I said. "It goes pretty fast."

The girl's eyes widened in terror, which clearly amused Wayne. "Yeah, it's horrible," he said. "It spins you around like crazy, tossing you about until your head's twirling so fast you don't know which way is up and which way is down."

133

"I d-don't like the sound of that," the girl said.

"It's not actually that bad," I began, but Wayne dug his elbow into me, shutting me up.

"It is. It's worse," he said. "Some people get so badly shaken their brain starts oozing out of their nose by the end. It's not pretty."

The girl's face turned a shade of lime-green. "I feel sick," she said. "I want to get off."

"Too late!" Wayne cackled, as the ride slowly began to spin.

Just before our cars went their separate ways, I offered the girl an encouraging smile. "You'll be fine. It doesn't last long," I told her, but she had her eyes shut and was gripping the bar, and I don't think she heard a word I said.

"That was pretty mean, Wayne," I said, as the car looped out in a circle and began to spin. "She was really scared."

"Oh, *she was really scared*," Wayne said, mimicking my voice. "So? What kind of baby gets scared on a ride like this?"

I was about to point out that he'd almost died of fright half a dozen times since we'd arrived at the park when I heard the retching. The cars were spinning quite quickly now, their momentum forcing us back into our seats. I looked round just in time to see the little girl's car spinning towards us and the girl herself opening her mouth wide.

BLEEURGH! A fountain of vomit erupted from her mouth and immediately spread out in a wide arc. Instinctively I ducked behind Wayne's jacket and heard the puke hit it like heavy rain.

I was saved from the sick but Wayne wasn't so lucky. The full force of the vomit-spray splattered across him. It hit his uniform and his face and plastered his fringe to his forehead. Wayne made a noise that was halfway between a gasp and a yelp, but it was drowned out by the screams of the younger kids around us.

135

The girl heaved again, ejecting the contents of her stomach just as the ride began to spin faster and faster. A perfect circle of vomit spread out around her and I ducked for cover behind Wayne's jacket again.

Once more, Wayne was too late to react. "Not again!" he cried as yet more puke rained down on him.

"Ew, that stinks," I said, covering my nose and mouth. The smell still found a way through, though, and as I watched the gloopy orange goo drip from Wayne's chin, I felt myself gag.

"Don't!" Wayne warned me, sliding to the far end of the car. "Don't you dare, Beaky!"

I swallowed a few times, bringing my urge to vomit back under control. "It's OK. I'm fine. I'm fine," I muttered, trying to think happy thoughts.

Wayne relaxed a little. "Just as well, because—"

BLEURGH!

Another boy with a weaker stomach than me threw up noisily. There were more screams as the vomit sprayed out in a three-hundred-and-sixty-degree spew spin and some shouted cursing from Wayne as he was plastered with the stuff for a third time.

Fearing a full-blown vomit fest, the ride operator hit the emergency stop and the cars slowed quickly to a halt.

As soon as the safety bar lifted, I jumped out of the way, narrowly avoiding the puddle of vomit that now sloshed about on the seats of our car. Wayne slowly stood up and waddled down from the ride, trying not to let any of his puke-stained clothes come into contact with the skin below.

The girl who'd started the vomit-fest reached the exit just before us. Despite being at the epicentre of the vomit explosion, she'd managed to stay remarkably clean. I was also completely spotless, thanks to Wayne's jacket.

"Are you OK?" I asked the girl. She began to nod, then retched and opened her mouth. I dodged sideways and the barf spray splattered all over Wayne's shoes. The girl took one look at Wayne's furious expression then turned and ran off in the direction of the toilets.

"Hey, Beaky."

Theo was walking along the path next to the ride with Duncan trotting along behind him like a faithful dog. When Theo saw Wayne, he stopped and looked him up and down. "You've got puke on you."

"Really?" Wayne snapped, scraping a blob of the stuff out of one of his ears. "I hadn't noticed."

He growled at me. "Give me your jumper."

"No chance!" I protested. "You can have your jacket back, though. It's probably ruined."

I jumped aside as Wayne tried to grab me. He was still trying not to let his puke-coated clothes touch him, so he was moving much more slowly than usual.

"Did you see a crisp packet?" I asked Theo. "Pickled onion."

Theo shook his head. "Not that I noticed."

I looked around, searching for any sign of the crisp packet. Wherever the wind had taken it, though, it was nowhere in sight.

Theo leaned in closer to me. "So, you're still alive, then?"

"Just," I said, eyeing Wayne warily in case he lunged again. "But as soon as he gets me alone, I'm done for. Unless Clumso gets him first."

"Clumso?"

"Doesn't matter," I said.

"Oh well, you should be safe for the next half-hour, anyway."

"How come?" I asked.

Theo held up his watch and tapped it. "It's lunchtime."

I stared at him blankly. "So?"

"So, we're supposed to meet up with the teachers near the entrance," Theo said.

I don't think I've ever been so happy to hear the word "teacher" in my life. I was safe for the next half-hour. After lunch it'd only be an hour or so until we all had to head for the bus to go home again. Maybe I'd survive my day with Wayne after all.

We all started walking back towards the entrance. Duncan stuck at Theo's side, keeping a safe distance from Wayne, who waddled and squelched along beside me, muttering under his breath.

"So, anything interesting to report?" Theo asked. I glanced at Wayne, who fired a warning glare right back at me. He mimed drawing his thumb across his throat and I wished more than ever before that I could tell a lie.

If I could lie, I could just say, "Nah, nothing really," and the conversation would be over, but the truth of it was we had got up to stuff I knew Theo would find interesting. Pretty much all of it made Wayne look like a big clown-fearing cry-baby, though, and I knew if I told Theo about it I'd never make it to lunch.

Just say no, just say no, just say no, I thought. As usual, though, my mouth had other ideas. "Yes!" I blurted. I shot Theo a pleading look. "But if I tell you, Wayne will snap me in half like a twig."

Theo looked from me to Wayne and back again. He shrugged. "Fair enough," he said, and he didn't ask me any more.

When we reached the picnic area, most of our group were already there, munching through their packed lunches. Mrs Rose rushed over to us almost immediately, looking us both up and down.

"How are things going with you two?" she asked, shooting me an accusing glare. "Is everything all…?" She stopped when the smell of vomit hit her. "What on earth happened?" she asked, covering her nose with a crinkled old piece of tissue.

"A little girl was sick on one of the rides," I said.

"Yeah, because Dylan made her sick," Wayne said.

"What? No, I didn't!" I spluttered. "What did I do, stick my fingers down her throat?"

Wayne visibly flinched, as if terrified I was about to hit him. *Man, he was good*. He quickly shook his head. "N-no, but you kept telling her about how fast it went and how scary it was. The poor girl was terrified."

I stared at him in disbelief, my mouth flapping open and closed like the animatronic Clumso's. "No, but… That's not… I mean…"

"Why am I not surprised?" Mrs Rose snapped.

She took Wayne's jacket from me, being careful not to get puke on her hands. "And I suppose you stole this off poor Wayne to protect yourself, did you?"

I began to protest but she silenced me with a wave of her hand. "I don't want to hear it, Dylan. You have no idea how angry I am right now." She handed Wayne his jacket. "Off you go to the toilet and get cleaned up, Wayne." She shot me a final glare. "And I'll deal with you later."

As Mrs Rose stormed off to deal with some other pupils who were play-fighting on one of the benches, Wayne slammed his ruined jacket into the bin beside us. "Don't go anywhere," he warned me. "And get working on my report."

He headed for the toilets, glancing back at me every few paces to make sure I hadn't made a run for it. I slumped down on to a low wall and Theo sat next to me. Duncan perched himself at the far end and started tucking into his lunch.

"Fun day, then?" Theo said, as we both took a bite of our sandwiches.

"You have no idea," I muttered. I glanced from side to side, then leaned in close. "But I think Madame Shirley's in the park."

Theo swallowed his bite of sandwich. "Wow. Really?" He took another bite and chewed slowly. "Who's Madame Shirley again?"

"The shop! The magic box," I whispered. "The woman who took away my ability to lie."

"Got you. Her. Right," Theo said. "What makes you think she's in the park?"

"I saw a crisp bag," I said.

Theo paused with his sandwich halfway to his mouth. "Is that the one you asked me about?"

I nodded. "Yep. Pickled onion."

"Oh. Well that definitely proves it," said Theo. "She's here all right."

"Keep an eye out for her," I said, even though I could tell he was being sarcastic. "She looks like a scarecrow who's recently had a surprise."

"Will do."

I was about to have another bite of my sandwich when Wayne appeared beside me. His face and hair were wet from where he'd obviously run his head under a tap and he'd made an effort to clean the vomit off his jumper and his trousers. It hadn't really worked very well, though, and now he looked damp and puke-stained, as opposed to just puke-stained.

He caught me by the arm and yanked me to my feet, scattering my lunch everywhere.

"Hey, watch it," I protested, bracing myself for a sneaky rabbit-punch to the stomach. When I saw Wayne's face, though, I knew he wasn't there to beat me up.

"He's found us. I don't know how, but he's found us," Wayne babbled.

He pointed across the plaza and there, thundering towards us with his curly orange hair blowing behind him, was Clumso the Clued-up Clown.

CHAPTER 10
SURELY NOT SHIRLEY?

We ran.

Wayne, still dripping wet, powered ahead, dragging me behind him. He drove straight through crowds of younger kids like they were skittles, scattering them in all directions.

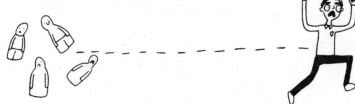

After a couple of minutes of frantic racing, Wayne slowed to a fast walk and released his grip on me.

"That was close," he wheezed. "He almost got us."

"What exactly do you think he's going to do if he does catch up with us?" I wondered. At most, I thought he'd bring us to a teacher and tell them what we – well, Wayne – had done. As I was already being blamed for forcing an eight-year-old to vomit on someone, getting shouted at for assaulting a clown didn't seem like that much of a big deal.

"Kill us and eat us, probably," Wayne said.

I started to laugh, then realized he was being deadly serious. "Um, I'm not sure he will."

Wayne nodded quickly. "That's what he does. My big brother told me years ago," he said.

"Ah. Right. I think maybe we've found the problem," I said. "I think your big brother might have been winding you up."

Wayne spun to face me, fists clenched, mouth snarling. "Are you calling my big brother a liar?"

I held up my hands, trying to calm him. "Yes. He's absolutely a liar," I said. "Or possibly insane." I flinched. "Which sounds bad when I say it out loud, I admit."

"My brother wouldn't lie to me about something like that. He's a good bloke and he told me that Clumso kills and eats people," Wayne said.

"When did he say this?" I asked.

"When I was four," Wayne told me. "Just before he went to jail."

I shrugged. There was clearly no point trying to reason with him. "We'd best keep out of his way, then."

GO TO
JAiL

"Ssh! Shut up! Don't say anything!" Wayne hissed. His furious glare turned into a beaming smile as he waved at two girls from our class who were passing nearby. "Hi, Chloe!" he called. "Hi, uh, other one."

Chloe Donovan was generally considered to be the most fanciable girl in our year. I didn't see it myself – I mean, she was no Miss Gavistock the dinner lady – but her blond curls, blue eyes and button nose seemed to do it for lots of the other boys. Wayne included, by the looks of him.

"Hey. How's it going? I didn't see you at lunch," Wayne said, bounding up to the girls like an excited puppy. He completely ignored Chloe's friend, Evie, but then Evie wasn't in to make-up and hair extensions and that kind of stuff and had probably grown used to being eclipsed by Chloe.

"Have lunch with those losers? I don't think so," Chloe said. She looked Wayne up and down. "And OMG, *ew*. What happened to you?"

"A kid threw up on him," I said. "Three times."

"Shut up, Beaky," Wayne threw me a warning look.

"It went in his hair and everything. I think a bit went in his mouth," I added, jumping back just in time to avoid getting a dead arm.

"Ew, that's revolting," Chloe said, practically sticking her nose in the air. "Come on, Evie," she said. "Let's go before they puke on us."

"We didn't puke on anyone!" I protested.

"I'd *never* puke on you, Chloe," Wayne blurted. "You know, unless you wanted me to." He looked shocked by the words coming out of his mouth, like they were projectile vomiting out of him and he couldn't stop it. "Why would you want me to do that? I mean, you wouldn't, would you? That would be mental. I wouldn't do it even if you asked me to. No way. I'm not going to puke on you and that's final."

Chloe and Evie both stared at him, open-mouthed. Wayne cleared his throat and gave a brief wave. "See you later."

"Smooth," I said as we watched them hurry away.

Wayne spun round and grabbed my jumper. "Why'd you tell her that stuff? About me being puked on."

"You stink of vomit," I wheezed through my narrowed windpipe. "She'd n-noticed before I'd said anything. B-besides, it was better that than I t-told her you fancy her."

"I do not!" Wayne growled, squeezing harder.

"Y-yes, you do," I croaked.

I held Wayne's gaze, and after a few more seconds of snarling he released his grip. I rubbed at my throat, gulping down lungfuls of air. "Don't worry about it," I said. "Pretty much everyone fancies her. She could have her pick of the boys in our year. Which means you probably don't have any chance. Sorry."

"You'd better not tell anyone," Wayne said.

"I probably will," I admitted. "I'll probably tell everyone."

Wayne started to lunge for me again, but then a crowd of old people rolled past on little motorized scooters. As the electric vehicles hummed quietly on their way, a couple of the grey-haired grannies gave us a wave.

"Check out the zombie invasion," Wayne muttered.

"What are they doing here?" I wondered. "I'm pretty sure none of them are still in primary school."

"And what, you think they remember anything they learned back then?" Wayne snorted. "Half of them probably don't remember their own name."

The scooters trundled across the park, headed for an area we hadn't explored yet. As I watched, one of them banked off to the left, leaving the rest of the group behind.

Slowly I stepped forwards, staring at the woman riding that scooter. I could only see the back of her head, but there was something very familiar about her startled-scarecrow hairstyle.

Could it be...?

The scooter stopped near *It's a Funny Old World* – a pedalo boat ride through an artificial cave, designed to teach kids about geography or nature or something. The woman sprang from her seat like she was twenty years old, then hurried for the entrance. *It's a Funny Old World* was the dullest ride in the park (which was really saying something), so the woman didn't have to waste any time queuing. If anything, the staff member at the entrance looked surprised to see someone approaching.

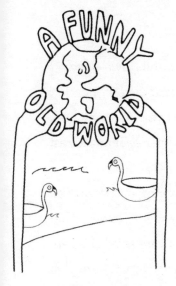

Just before the woman ducked inside, she glanced back at me and I got a better look at her face. Her *very familiar* face.

"Madame Shirley," I whispered. It was her, I was sure of it.

I set off running, leaving Wayne somewhere behind as I called to the old woman at the top of my voice. "Hey! Wait! Stop!"

She was already through the entrance, though, and either she didn't hear or she was ignoring my shouts.

If the man staffing the ride entrance was surprised to have one visitor, he was even more shocked when I came running up. "Can I help you?" he asked.

"I want to go on the ride," I said hurriedly.

"Really?" he asked, frowning. He jabbed a thumb towards the archway behind him. "On this?"

I nodded and the man shrugged, then stepped aside.

"Knock yourself out," he said.

I was about to rush through when Wayne caught my arm.

"Where do you think you're going?" he demanded.

"Let go, Wayne. I'm going on this ride," I said.

"No, you're not," Wayne growled. He said it with such menace in his voice that I almost caved in and let him lead me away. But then I spotted something over Wayne's shoulder and I knew I'd won.

I pulled my arm away sharply. "Yes, Wayne, I am. I'm going on this ride and you're not going to stop me."

Wayne stepped closer. "What? You think I'm scared of you?"

"No," I admitted. "But I think you're scared of him."

I pointed past Wayne to where Clumso the

Clued-up Clown was half running, half waddling across the park. From the way he was looking around, I didn't think he'd spotted us, but it was only a matter of time.

"So you can either stay out here and deal with Clumso or come on this ride," I said. "Your call."

I turned away and marched through the archway to where the pedalo boats were tied up. My heart was thumping against my ribs but Wayne didn't scare me nearly as much as the thought of losing Madame Shirley did.

"Hurry up!" I told him, jumping into the little red and green boat. Muttering angrily, Wayne clambered into the seat next to me and my legs pumped furiously as I powered us onwards into the dark.

CHAPTER 11

BOAT CHASE

The tunnel we pedalled into was almost completely in darkness, except for the strips of light below the surface of the shallow water showing us which direction to go. The glow rippled on the walls of the tunnel, which had been designed to make the place look like a rocky cave.

I could hear the splashing of Madame Shirley's boat somewhere in the gloom up ahead and pedalled faster, trying to catch up. Wayne sat back, letting me do all the work and occasionally scooping up a handful of water to flick in my face.

"What d'you want to go on this thing for?" he asked. "It's rubbish."

I tried to reply but I was too out of breath. My leg muscles were already burning but I powered the pedals round, faster and faster. Up ahead, I caught a glimpse of the other boat slicing gracefully through the water, then it was lost round a bend in the river.

Huffing and puffing, I gave chase. I could still hear the water lapping against the sides of Madame Shirley's boat but now I could hear other sounds, too. Singing. Laughter. And the whirring of animatronics.

Suddenly I remembered exactly what the *It's a Funny Old World* ride was all about.

"Um, you might want to shut your eyes," I said, as we banked round the bend and straight into Wayne's worst nightmare.

Thousands of doll-sized Clumsos lined the banks of the river. They were all wearing little costumes based on the national dress of various countries. There were Clumsos in lederhosen, Clumsos in kilts and bearded Clumsos wearing turbans.

An Inuit Clumso was sitting on a block of ice, dangling a fishing rod into the water. Behind him, a matador Clumso was being chased round in circles by a snorting plastic bull. At some point, someone had clearly decided the whole thing would be completely adorable, but as a thousand tiny robot clowns spun their heads our way I very nearly lost bladder control myself.

All the Clumsos were lit from below, casting their shiny plastic faces into dark, shadowy masks. Only the red noses and grins were visible on most of them, their mouths snapping open and closed as they sang:

Wherever you may go,
There's a Clumso!

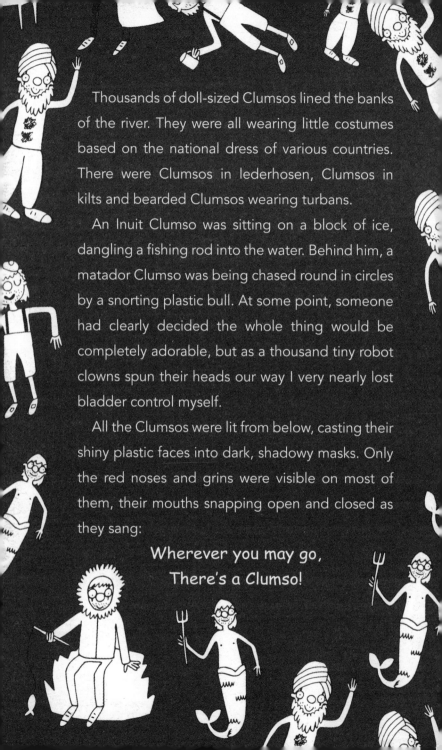

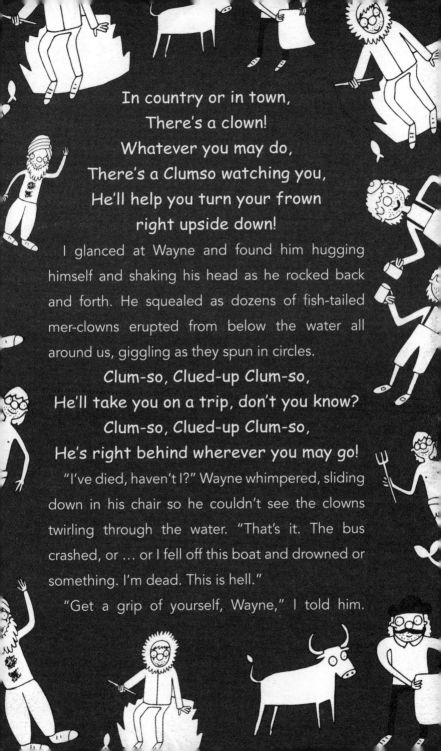

In country or in town,
There's a clown!
Whatever you may do,
There's a Clumso watching you,
He'll help you turn your frown
right upside down!

I glanced at Wayne and found him hugging himself and shaking his head as he rocked back and forth. He squealed as dozens of fish-tailed mer-clowns erupted from below the water all around us, giggling as they spun in circles.

Clum-so, Clued-up Clum-so,
He'll take you on a trip, don't you know?
Clum-so, Clued-up Clum-so,
He's right behind wherever you may go!

"I've died, haven't I?" Wayne whimpered, sliding down in his chair so he couldn't see the clowns twirling through the water. "That's it. The bus crashed, or … or I fell off this boat and drowned or something. I'm dead. This is hell."

"Get a grip of yourself, Wayne," I told him.

"It's nothing to freak out about. It's just several hundred mechanical clowns wearing traditional costumes and, in the case of that one," I said, pointing to a tartan-clad Clumso wielding a broadsword, "carrying traditional weapons."

I nodded towards his feet. "The faster we pedal, the faster we can get through it."

Wayne was too far gone to pedal, though. He cowered in his seat, covering his head with his hands and mumbling incoherently. I could just make out Madame Shirley's boat up ahead. From where I was sitting it didn't look like she was even pedalling, yet her boat was slicing easily through the water, pulling ahead with every second that passed.

"Come on, Wayne, I need you to pedal!" I yelped.

Wayne shook his head. "C-can't move," he whimpered.

Over the high-pitched singing and giggling

of the robo-clowns, I heard another sound. It was the splashing of another pedalo, and it was coming from behind us.

Still pumping with my legs, I craned my neck round to see who was behind me. There, to my surprise, was the real Clumso. He was pedalling hard and using one of his big shoes to row with.

"It's Clumso," I said. "He's coming."

Wayne shot me a dirty look through a gap in his fingers. "No he isn't."

"He is!" I insisted. "He's chasing us."

"You're lying," said Wayne, but there was a note of panic in his voice that was hard to miss.

"Why does no one ever believe me?" I sighed. "Just look!"

Hesitantly, Wayne leaned forward in his chair, then turned his head for just a tiny fraction of a second before facing front again.

"See him?" I asked.

"No," Wayne mumbled.

"You didn't look properly, did you?" I said.

"I did look properly!"

"Look again!"

"Fine!"

Taking a steadying breath, Wayne turned. He looked over my left shoulder at the river behind us. "There's no one there," he said.

"What?" I said. "But he was right—"

THUMP.

Clumso's boat bumped into ours, just to the left of Wayne. "Got you!" Clumso hissed, as Wayne let out a scream so high-pitched only dogs could hear it.

Kicking in panic, Wayne's feet found the pedals and he pumped his legs. The pedals under my feet moved, too, spinning so quickly I could barely keep up. Watched by the glassy eyes of hundreds of dancing clown dolls, our pedalo began to pull ahead.

"Faster! Pedal faster!" Wayne hollered, but my feet had slipped from the pedals and they were

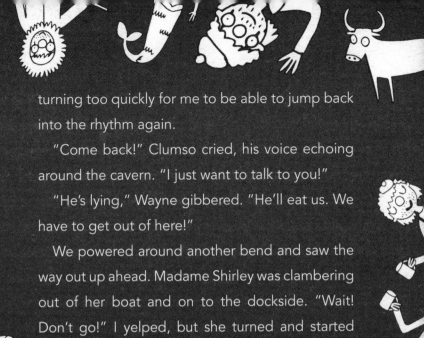

turning too quickly for me to be able to jump back into the rhythm again.

"Come back!" Clumso cried, his voice echoing around the cavern. "I just want to talk to you!"

"He's lying," Wayne gibbered. "He'll eat us. We have to get out of here!"

We powered around another bend and saw the way out up ahead. Madame Shirley was clambering out of her boat and on to the dockside. "Wait! Don't go!" I yelped, but she turned and started strolling towards the exit.

Determined to catch her, I managed to find the pedals and we both kicked furiously, gritting our teeth as I chased Madame Shirley and Wayne fled from Clumso the Clued-up Clown.

When we were less than a metre from the dock, Wayne stood up, almost tipping the pedalo over, and hurled himself towards dry land.

"What are you doing?" I cried, in disbelief as his legs pulled in opposite directions. For a moment, he seemed to be leaning at an impossible angle, frantically flapping his arms. Then, with a *splash*, he hit the water.

He thrashed around in panic, shouting, "I'm drowning! I'm drowning!" before finding he could stand 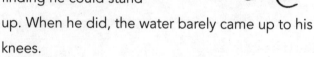 up. When he did, the water barely came up to his knees.

I smiled weakly at him. "Well, at least the rest of the sick's been washed off."

Realizing Clumso was closing fast, Wayne scrambled up on to the dock and sprinted towards the exit. With a pretty skilful bit of manoeuvring (if I do say so myself), I brought the boat in close to the edge and hopped out.

I blinked as I raced out of the dark tunnel into the light of the outside. Shielding my eyes, I scanned the park for Madame Shirley, desperately trying to pick her out from the crowd.

"Come on, where are you?" I muttered. "Where are you?"

There! She was sitting on her scooter by the *Gravity Drop*, leaning back to take in all of the twisting metal staircase that led up to the top. I hurried over, calling her name as I drew closer.

"Madame Shirley! Madame Shirley!"

She didn't turn. It wasn't until I clattered up behind her that she gave a little jerk that suggested she'd heard me.

"Hello, dear. Can I help you?" The old woman turned to face me and I felt my heart drop to somewhere around my knees. There was a bit of a resemblance, but up close it was obvious I'd made a mistake.

"You're not Madame Shirley," I told her. "You're just an old woman with mad hair."

The woman looked a little uncertain, but nodded and smiled. "Er... Madame who, dear?"

"She looks like you but has a magic shop," I said. "Have you seen her?"

The old woman's faint eyebrows furrowed. "I don't think so."

"Pickled onion crisps!" I said.

"I'm sorry?"

"She had loads of pickled onion crisps. And a box that stops you being able to lie."

The old lady looked at me blankly. "Um ... can't say that's ringing a bell. Never been fond of crisps, myself. Get stuck in my false teeth."

I pointed accusingly at her. "Your pedalo was moving by magic!"

"It was an electric one," the woman said. She patted herself on the thigh. "Legs aren't what they used to be."

"Oh," I said, lowering my arm again. "Yeah, that makes sense."

The woman rummaged in her pocket. "Mint?"

she asked, holding a crumpled paper bag out to me. "They're extra strong."

I took one. The fact she wasn't Madame Shirley was a huge disappointment, so I thought I might as well get a mint out of it.

"Thanks," I said, popping it in my mouth.

"Well, cheerio, dear," the woman said, rolling off on her scooter. "I hope you find your friend."

I gave her a half-hearted little wave and was about to head in the opposite direction when Wayne's voice growled in my ear.

"Hey, well done," he said.

"For what?" I asked, not daring to turn round.

Wayne nudged me towards the *Gravity Drop* entrance. At the bottom of the steps, a chain had been clipped in place, along with a little sign announcing the ride would re-open in 15 minutes.

"You found a closed ride," Wayne said. "It'll be nice and quiet up there."

My throat went dry. My legs shook with panic. This was it – Wayne had me cornered.

With a quick check around to make sure no one was watching, he shoved me towards the chain. "Get up the stairs," he said.

And with that, we began to climb.

CHAPTER 12
CAUGHT BY CLUMSO

At the top of the stairs was the *Gravity Drop* itself – a square room with glass walls and a dozen or so straps hanging from the ceiling. Wayne pushed me inside and my legs were so tired from the climb I almost fell over.

"Wow, those stairs were hard work," I puffed.

Wayne looked at my empty hands. "Where's my report?"

Oh no! The reports. "I must've left them on the pedalo," I realized.

"What?"

"It's OK, I hadn't written anything on yours anyway," I said truthfully. "And all I'd written on mine was about you beating up Clumso and crying on the train ride."

If I thought that was going to defuse the situation, I was wrong.

Wayne advanced, fists clenched. "I wasn't crying," he spat. "It was a dust allergy!"

"You were definitely crying," I said, then I winced. "I didn't mean to say that. It just came out. Like that wee you did when Clumso turned up in Year Six."

That did it. Wayne shoved me in the chest and I stumbled back towards one of the big windows. "I'm going to kill you," he said, so matter-of-factly that I actually believed him.

"Hey, easy, Wayne," I said, sliding along the window and trying to get away from him. "You don't want to end up in jail like your brother."

Wayne's already dark expression darkened even

further. He started advancing then stopped and looked uneasily down at the floor. There were two large glass panels in it, giving a clear view of the ground below. Wayne peered  down at them for a few moments, then his head snapped up.

"You're scared of heights," I said.

"I told you, I'm not scared of nothing!" he growled. He nervously licked his lips, swallowed hard, then made a grab for me.

I ducked just in time to avoid his grasping fingers. He advanced on me as I backed away across the room.

"We can talk about this," I said. "This doesn't have to end with anyone getting hurt. Especially me."

"Do you know how hard I've worked to make all the teachers think I'm one of the good guys?" Wayne asked, shuffling across the floor and giving the glass panels a wide berth. "Do you know how much effort that takes?"

"A lot?" I guessed.

Wayne nodded. "That's right. A lot. They all think I'm the perfect student, so how is it going to look when I don't turn in my report? It's going to blow my cover, isn't it?"

"I don't know. Maybe. A bit," I babbled, still backing off.

"So you're going to tell them you threw it away," Wayne said. "And that you pushed me into the water."

"I can't say that," I told him.

"You'd better!"

"No, I can't. It's like I tried to tell you earlier – I can't tell a lie. Something happened to me at the weekend – I can't really explain it, because I don't understand it, but now I can't lie."

Wayne stopped advancing and narrowed his eyes. "I don't believe you," he said.

I sighed. "No one ever does. But it's true," I said. "You could say those things, though. You could say

I chucked away your work and pushed you in the water. I mean, you were probably going to, anyway, because you're a horrible creep, but—"

My back bumped against the glass on the other side of the room and I realized I had nowhere left to go. With a final few unsteady steps, Wayne was right in front of me. I tried to slide sideways but he slammed a hand against the glass wall, blocking my escape.

I swallowed. "If the teacher sees me with a black eye, she'll know it was you."

Wayne grinned, showing his yellow teeth. "Don't worry. I won't leave a mark. I've done this lots of times before."

"Oh. Well, that's reassuring," I whimpered. "At least I'm in the hands of an expert."

I braced myself for the pain, then spotted a shape heaving itself up the stairs. A colourful shape. With jiggling pom-poms.

"C-Clumso," I whispered.

Wayne sneered. "Yeah, like I'm going to fall for that," he began. But then came the unmistakable slapping sound of Clumso's massive shoes on the floor. Or rather, just one massive shoe. Clumso seemed to have lost the other one. And that was the least of his problems.

His orange wig was peeling off at his temples, revealing a closely cropped skinhead below. Either water or sweat had mixed in with his make-up, which now ran down his face in streaks of purple, green and white.

Clumso's satin trousers were ripped at both knees and I could see nasty-looking grazes on his skin below. One of his pom-pom buttons had fallen off and there was something else missing, too: his smile. Clumso the Clued-up Clown did *not* look happy.

Wayne turned then immediately pressed himself up against the glass beside me.

"There you are," Clumso said, limping towards us.

"I've been chasing you little thugs all day. Thought you'd give old Clumso the slip, eh? Thought you'd managed to get away?"

The more I saw of Clumso, the more terrifying he was becoming. He'd been mildly unsettling when we'd first met him that morning and he'd given me a fright on the pedalo ride. Now, though, he looked like the deranged villain of a horror movie, with Wayne and me playing his latest victims.

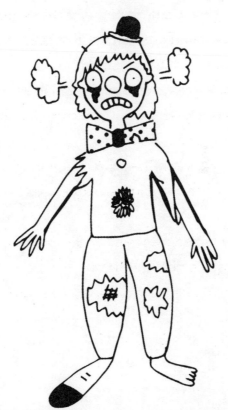

Wayne was trying to say something but all that was coming out was a high-pitched croak. Clumso dragged himself closer. Four metres away. Three. Two. My blood whooshed through my veins. Wayne was right. This was it. I was about to be killed and eaten by a theme park clown mascot.

Clumso stopped and leaned down so his red nose was just centimetres away from us. "I've just got one thing to say to you two," he whispered, his eyes going slowly from Wayne to me and back again. "Cows have four stomachs."

Wayne and I both started to scream, then stopped. We glanced at one another. "W-what?" I stammered.

Clumso leaned back. "I told you, I've got to give you a fact. Cows have four stomachs. There you go."

With a final glare at us, he turned and began limping back towards the stairs. I had just begun to relax when he spun round, his face a mask of fury.

"HOW MANY STOMACHS DOES A COW HAVE?" he roared.

"F-four!" Wayne and I both yelped at the same time.

Clumso smiled. "Well remembered," he said, then he winked at us and carried on to the stairs. "Man, I am so quitting this stupid job," he muttered, beginning the slow climb back down.

Wayne and I stood there in silence, both breathing heavily, still pressed against the glass. It took me almost a full minute to find my voice. "Well, I suppose that could've gone a lot worse," I said.

And then, without warning, the doors in front of the stairs slammed shut and the whole room plunged towards the ground, accompanied by the high-pitched giggle of Clumso the Clued-up Clown.

HE HEE HE HE HEE HE HEE HE HEE

CHAPTER 13

HOME TIME

I'd love to say it was just Wayne who screamed like a five-year-old as the *Gravity Drop* fell. That would be a lie, though. The truth was that we both squealed and clung to each other in terror as we plummeted towards the ground.

When the brakes kicked in and the ride slowed to a stop, we quickly released our grip on one another and looked in opposite directions, trying to pretend the last few seconds hadn't happened.

The door slid open and we stepped outside, just in time to see Mrs Rose striding past. "There you are. Come on, it's home time. Back to the bus."

I almost cheered. I had done it. I had somehow survived the day with Wayne without him beating me to a pulp. I was safe!

"Just coming, Miss," Wayne said, smiling sweetly. He waited until she had pulled ahead, then turned to me. "As soon as we're off that bus and back at school, you're dead."

OK, so maybe not *that* safe.

We made our way back to the coach and everyone rushed to pile on. Theo and I sat down in the same seats we'd sat in earlier.

"You survived then," Theo said.

"For now," I mumbled. "But Wayne's going to kill me when we get back to school."

"Ah," said Theo. "That's unfortunate. Can't you just tell the teacher?"

I shook my head. "They'll never believe me. They think I've been bullying him!"

"Suppose," Theo said. "Shame there isn't a way they could see him like we do."

"Yeah," I sighed, then I felt a stirring somewhere at the back of my brain, like a memory was waving its arms about and trying to attract my attention.

See him like we do. See him like we do.

I sat bolt upright in the seat. "Wait! That's it!"

Frantically, I began to pat the front of my school jumper. "Where is it? Where is it?"

"Where's what?" Theo asked. He edged away. "Is it a spider? It's not a spider, is it?"

"No, it's— Aha!" My hand pressed down on the circle of plastic and glass. The camera was still on my jumper!

Taking out my phone, I checked the open

apps and – yes! – there it was. The app had been running since last night, recording everything that had happened.

"We've got him," I gasped. "We've got him. Attacking Clumso, threatening me, making that little girl puke. We've got everything! I can show Mrs Rose."

Theo took the phone from me. "I've got a better idea," he said. "The Journeyman 8228 really is an impressive coach," he said.

I rolled my eyes. "Not this again."

"No, you'll like this," he said, tapping at my screen. "As well as the extra leg room, deluxe toilets and all that other stuff, it's got something else, too."

"And what's that?"

Theo grinned and nodded at the TV, which was showing boring countryside scenes. "Bluetooth," said Theo. He tapped my screen and the image on the TV changed.

All the kids were on board now and Mrs Rose was pacing along the aisle, doing her head count. She stopped when Wayne's voice came blasting out of the TV.

"Leave me alone, you big freak!"

All eyes went to the screen. The footage was shaky, but everyone could clearly see Wayne just as he booted Clumso in the shins and shoved him to the ground.

"Here, give it to me," I whispered, taking the phone from Theo. I skipped forwards to the train ride. At the corner of the screen it was just possible to make out Wayne with his hands over his head.

"This is the worst thing that's ever happened in

the world," the on-screen Wayne sobbed.

Around us, a few kids began to giggle. I skipped forwards again and Wayne's sneer filled the screen. "Better get writing. Fill my report out. Say that ride was lame," he said through the TV's tinny speakers. "Too slow and boring. And if you say anything about me crying, I'll kill you."

Mrs Rose turned and looked over at Wayne. "Wayne?" she said. "What is this?"

Wayne opened his mouth to speak but his lies had run out. I skipped ahead again, letting everyone see Wayne tormenting the girl on the ride then lingering on him being splattered with her puke. A big cheer went up at that.

WAHOO YAY!

"Who is playing this?" Mrs Rose demanded. My hand went up all by itself.

"Me, Miss," I said.

She rounded on me, looking furious. "How dare you, Dylan? Recording a fellow pupil without their consent is a direct violation of the school's rules and privacy policy. You're in *very* big trouble."

"You tell him, Miss," Wayne said.

Mrs Rose tutted. "Oh, shut up, Wayne. Drop the act. I'll deal with you when we get back to school," Mrs Rose snapped, startling Wayne with her tone. She held a hand out to me. "Give me the camera."

"But—"

"Don't make me ask again, Dylan," she said. "That's my only warning."

I got the feeling she wasn't kidding. Even Theo gulped. "I'd give her the camera, Beaky."

Reluctantly I unclipped the spy camera and passed it to her. She slipped it straight into her pocket without looking at it. "If I ever catch you with anything like that again you'll be facing expulsion. Is that clear?"

"Yes, Miss," I said. "I didn't actually realize I had it on."

Mrs Rose shook her head. "More lies. Surprise, surprise," she said, then she about-turned and pressed the power button on the TV, just as Wayne splashed face-first into the water.

"Great. Something else she thinks I'm lying about," I muttered, sinking back down into my seat. "Guess I should be used to that by now."

Theo shrugged. "It's not all bad. Wayne's going to be in big trouble when we get to school, so he won't be able to beat you up."

That was true. I'd saved myself from a beating. Of course he'd catch up with me eventually and he'd be even angrier by then, but I didn't need to worry about that now.

The front doors of the bus hissed closed and the engine rumbled into life beneath us. The bus had just started to creep forwards when Theo nudged me. "Here, Beaky," he said. "Who's that waving at you?"

I leaned over, looking through the window to where he was pointing. An elderly woman with hair like a startled scarecrow and a long, rainbow scarf stood on the pavement. At first, I thought it was the same old woman I'd chased, but when she reached into her pocket and pulled out a packet of pickled onion crisps I looked at her more closely.

"It's her! It's Madame Shirley," I yelped, just as the coach sped up and pulled away.

I leaped to my feet but Mrs Rose hissed at me to sit down!

"No, but I have to speak to that old woman!" I yelped. "I think she did a magic spell on me."

Mrs Rose glared at me. The coach pulled out of the car park and on to the motorway, and I flopped back down into my seat. It was too late. Madame Shirley had been right there and I'd missed my chance.

Still, if she was at the park then she wasn't in Poland or America or North Korea. She was somewhere nearby and that meant I could find her again.

As the coach picked up speed, a smile spread across my face. I'd exposed Wayne for what he really was, I'd discovered Madame Shirley was still in the country and, as a bonus, I'd learned quite a bit about the UK rail network.

"You know what, Theo, today hasn't been too bad," I said.

"That's good." Theo smiled. "Because tomorrow will probably be much worse."

"You think?"

Theo nodded. "Oh yeah. And not just tomorrow. You've got the school play coming up, that inter-schools contest thing with the debates and the team-building exercises, all that stuff." He shook his head. "Man, I'm glad I'm not you."

"Well, thanks for those reassuring words," I said.

"Sorry, Beaky, but it's the truth," Theo said. "Much as I hate to say it, I think you've got some pretty rough times ahead."

"Yeah," I groaned. "Yeah, you're probably right."

As it turns out, he was right.

But he didn't know the half of it.

Want to know how Beaky lost the ability to lie?
Then read this one!

BEAKY MALONE

WORLD'S GREATEST LIAR

?!@*?!

Just lost the
ability to lie!

BARRY
HUTCHISON

Illustrated by
KATIE ABEY

And look out
for Book 3,
coming soon!

A night in the wilderness
with Wayne? Gah!
How am I going to survive?